I0527410

No Zappa

Suki Tamarind

P&C Itsmybook 2012

Front cover painting
P&C Bob Mgintie 2010

Portrait of Suki
P&C Yoyo Frangipani 2010

Chapter One

In which our main protagonists re-acquaint themselves with a few things, including each other.

"For fuck's sake, we are here now, will you just make the best of it."

"Janice, I said I wasn't keen, may have even mentioned it once or twice."

"And on and on."

"Who's organised this anyway?"

"Oh that would be Mandy, she won't be here yet, the poor dear needs to make an entrance. Just wait till you see her."

Barbara had been lured, against her better judgment (is there any other kind of luring?) to the end of term/beginning of the summer party. Bloody teachers, she hated them, she was one but she'd never been keen on the rest. It was being held in the upper room of a pub on the edge of town. Quite nice really, evidently they held fetish parties here. There were funny little marks on the metal pillars and lots of things one could be tied to, if one so wished.

"Well Janice, you would be the one to know."

An heroic buffet had been laid out and what looked like a bunch of teachers desperately trying to appear cool had just finished their sound check. Janice was checking out the drummer in a big way.

"Oh dear, so that's why we are here."

"Oh yes, can you imagine the sweat?"

"Janice you are a deeply sick individual, deeply, deeply sick. But why, just tell me, why am I here?"

"Don't want to appear too desperate."

"You already know him."

"No, I know the bloke with the green guitar."

"That's a bass."

"Come on Barb you haven't been out for ages, or ever even."

"Brilliant and now I get to watch you devour your victim."

"Victim!"

"The poor chap does not stand a chance."

"Yum, yum, and he's not a teacher!"

"What does he do then?"

"Don't know, don't care, can you imagine, a real person."

"Like wow man! Janice you are so, just so…"

"So what?"

"Exactly, come on smile on full beam, here you go."

Janice launched into overdrive, loads of talking and giggling at every passing remark, and even more hair flicking. After the initial skirmish Barbara's flabber was gasted.

"Since when did you care about what kind of bass pedal he used, since when did you even know what a bass pedal was?"

"Went to a music shop; forward planning you see. He shall be mine."

"Janice, he's a bloke; just turn up, that would do it. He's drummer; that barely registers as human, he's hardly Brad Pitt."

"It would seem that I have a higher regard for the male species that you my dear."

"Well you are a fucking idiot."

"And look at the state of you."

Barbara gave her the evil eye; she was good at the evil eye. Barbara could kill plants with her evil eye. Suddenly there was a considerable fluster and even a bit of a bluster, the very sort of fluster and bluster that one would expect to occur if there was a definite entrance being made.

"Good god, who do they belong to?"

"All hers, and she has the receipt to prove it, got it framed on her kitchen wall."

"They are a bit.."

"Humongous, look bloody silly to me, but each to their own, she's had them a couple of years now, evidently when she first got them she would wander round pubs getting men to grope her, went on for months."

Barbara then realised where she had seen the woman before, Barbie doll incarnate had shown up at a most inopportune moment. A huge feeling of oh shit crept through her entire, and surgically unaltered, body.

"You ok?"

"I'm good, why?"

"You just went white, and a little green."

"Ok, how long do you recon it's going to take you to pull Bonzo there." Barbara gestured to the silicon centred melee that the drummer had become a part of, she was impressed that he at least had the dignity not to stare directly at the puppies as they took their constitutional. Then " he" walked past, she hadn't seen "him" for two years, he didn't even acknowledge the poor mutts; he just walked over to the stage area and started looking at a guitar. Its owner handed it to him and plugged it in. Barbara had recognised the back of his head and his walk and he still had that tattered jacket. She almost got round to thinking of doing a runner when he stopped playing, looked at her and smiled. The guitar was returned to its rightful and he came over and said hello.

"And a deathly hush fell over Gotham City."

"Well I feel awkward, oh sod it; I take it that you are all well and everything in your life is wonderful, still a shit guitarist though."

"Oh thanks a bunch, not my guitar, he just wanted me to look at it, sort it out a bit."

"Andrew stop making excuses, this is a party you know, you always were a bit scruffy, but, come on."

4

"I was doing some painting."

"Never have guessed, get any of it on the picture?"

"Oh, ha, ha. Anyway it's next years black."

And then Mandy appeared, with all the pomp and ceremony that that entailed. A huge fuss was made, and she made a huge fuss of everyone, she was determined to get the most from her extra appendages. When Andy was finally let go he had a smear of red on his unshaven cheek.

"I thought you didn't do parties."

"I don't I'm just here for the band, speaking of which, you could have got a good one."

"Andy I told you, I need someone who isn't going to upset and offend, the last time I saw your mob, you were dressed as a rabbit and the bass player fell over drunk during the third song."

"He got up again!"

"It was Sunday lunch time."

"Good point, but I did sort that shit out for you." Andy pointed at the huge banner over the buffet.

"That does not excuse you from attending."

"Well I'm here now, evidently not dressed for it." She looked at Barbara and an introduction was made.

"The Barbara! Oh my god, oops sorry."

"Thanks."

Mandy turned back to Barbara.

"You realise no one can ever compete with you." Then Turned to Andy "And I brought my little friend along for you."

"Oh not again!"

"She's nice, look over there." Mandy waved and an incredibly cute girlie waved back. "Gotta go, hi Janice, got your teeth into him yet?" She looked at Barbara, "I had to go into a music shop with her, bass pedals, honestly who cares?" Janice got the full flutter treatment and tried to introduce Barbara. "Oh we're old friends, see ya later." And the whirlwind left.

"Didn't know you knew her?"

Barbara just shook her head. Janice looked at Andy.

"Let me guess: it's the new black."

Barbara took a deep breath and introduced them.

"The Andy!"

"Piss off, look there he is, search and destroy, go,go,go."

Janice looked a bit bewildered.

"Go away!"

"Why are you covered in paint?"

"Told you, what did she mean "The Andy"?"

"And what was "no one can compete with me" all about."

"You know, love of my life, the wonder of you, all that crap."

"What!"

"Well sort of, nearly, might have been."

"Bollox, we never even went out, let alone, well you know."

"That's probably it, forever a perfect notion."

"Still full of shit then."

"I was under the impression that we kind of sort of nearly once were going to go out, I had a clean shirt and everything, no paint. But alas a certain person failed to show. Don't suppose you would care to tell me what happened. I thought, well never mind. I thought we were good, we could have been, you know. What did I do, not do, did I mention the clean shirt?"

"Why are you assuming it was you?"

"Coz you are perfect so it must have been me, anyway I'm a Leo remember, it's always…"

"All about me."

"Oh dear, look she smiles, I remember that smile, oh poo, I seem to have gone all theatrical darling."

"You didn't really do anything."

"Just changed your mind?"

Barbara shrugged. "Sort of."

"What are you giggling about?"

"No matter, did you really dress up as a rabbit?"

"Of course, why not?"

"I saw your mob at some bikers do, about a year ago, you were good, looked like you were making it all up as you went along, still good."

"Very good subject change, I thought I saw you, I waved."

"I know."

"Come on two years; what happened?"

"Does it matter?"

"Does to me, come on we could have been married and divorced and you could be a single mum by now, could well be, no, didn't think so. Or we could have just had a big fight and never spoken again, or we could have started a wonderful relationship and walked hand in hand along moonlight beaches and stuff."

"And stuff."

"Sounds good to me."

"Moonlight beaches, sounds good, you realise that you cant actually get further from the sea than we are at this very moment."

"There's always Norfolk."

"Terribly, terribly flat"

"Or Spain."

"Mmm..ok here goes.."

Then the band started and everyone was expected to dance. Barbara and Andy danced out the door and down the stairs and into the bar.

Barbara bought two pints of cider and asked.

"Why are you covered in paint?"

"And for the third time, I was doing some painting. I had setup for an evening of artistic brilliance, pile of DVDs, a six pack of Skol and the artistic genius within."

"Such class, a six pack of Skol, wow!"

"Then idiot boy turns up and drags me here."

"Idiot boy?"

"Mandy's husband, idiot boy, says I have to be here, can't see what difference it makes myself, what possible difference could it make? She really gets on my tits, that bloody woman."

"Sets you up with friends though."

"Only sometimes, piss off."

"How long have they been married?"

"Five, six years ish, I don't know."

"Hand in hand along moonlight beaches."

"At midnight."

"Makes all the difference. I do so hate to be judgemental but judging by the state of your attire I take it there is no specific significant other at present."

"She could be away for the weekend."

"But she's not."

"Nope, last one buggered of a few months ago, but at least she told me why."

"Let me guess, is it because you are a twat?"

"That was the gist of it, but it took two and a half hours and a complete character assassination to get to the point."

"It's not like you hide it, I mean she must have known when she met you."

"You'd think."

"How long did it last?"

"Six months."

"So how come she's not your long lost love."

"Coz you are."

"Rubbish."

"True, I've decided, there has to be one so it's you."

"But we never.."

"Exactly."

"So it's pure."

"As the driven show, anyway it's in the book."

"What book?"

"The rule book."

"There's a rule book. I've never read it."

"Big shiny thing, pink cover. Page one rule one, don't shit on your friends."

"Ha, ha, hand in hand at midnight."

"Moonlight beaches and everything. How about you?"

"Me!"

"You know."

"Sort of."

"Yeah or nay."

"He's married."

"Oh dear, Kids?"

"Three."

"Oh dearie dear. So Babs you are now, a mistress."

"Do not call me that, never call me that. Suppose I was really."

"Does he keep you in a magnificent apartment and whisk you off for filthy weekends?"

"No, he took me to Barcelona once but we had a big fight and I went off and got shit faced with seven Irish girls on a hen night, stayed at their hotel."

"So, and again so, when he leaves his wife will you become the wicked stepmother?"

"Piss off, you can be so horrid, well I did think, at one point he might leave his wife, but then she got up the duff again, stop laughing, it just gets worse. Anyway you and miss perfect, hand in hand on sun kissed beaches."

"Pretty much."

"Was it good?"

"Brilliant, thought about you though."

"Rubbish."

"I did, not all night."

"Not when you were shagging her."

"No, not then, but when we were pissing about, well after midnight on moonlight beaches, I thought; Babs, don't hit me, would have loved this."

"Then you fucked her."

"Oh yeah, but that's not the point. See the point is that we, us, you know me and you, spent shit loads of time together, stuck in traffic and stuff and we used to talk a lot, a lot of bollocks admittedly but a lot all the same, so when ever I see something that I think you would like I say to my self "Barbara would have loved that" or hated it or what ever, and I never call you Babs even when I'm talking to my self. For example, ceramics fair last week, little yellow submarine, you would have liked that."

"Yes I saw that and I though "Andy would have loved the planes, and did you see the green dogs."

"Oh yeah, are you going to tell me what happened?"

"Does it matter?"

"I'd just like to know, unless it's going to involve another character assassination."

"If you had called again I would probably have told you."

"I called three times, the last time you said you would do me for harassment."

"I may not have actually meant that."

"You and the married bloke; you going to see it through?"

"No."

"Seems pretty definite."

"It is, had enough, gotta go. It has been a bit convenient, you know, my time's my own, I can pretty much pencil him in at any time I like."

"Pencil him in?"

"Yes, I've always been a romantic little soul."

"Alright Miss Romance, let's go up the road to the Pit and pretend it's two years ago."

"That's just dumb."

"Not to me."

"Why would you want to do that?"

"Because you kissed me once and I want to do it again"

"Never kissed you."

"The day before you so cruelly stood me up and broke my heart."

"Oh yes, and I wasn't even drunk."

"That's my favourite ever kiss."

"Oh just, oh you nearly had me there, but I remember your eyes."

"No really, best ever."

"Oh this is worse than a Sandra Bullock movie."

"No, it's true, when ever I'm alone and need something to push it over the edge, I just think of that kiss and wooosh!"

"That's disgusting, do you?"

"No, that's what the Internet's for, but it is without doubt the best kiss I have ever been on the receiving end of. Tell you what, just kiss me now and if it's crap we can go back to the party."

"What so you can cop of with that little porn star the delightful Mandy has set you up with? It fact, just to stop you, get that down your neck, come on let's go."

Andy tried to explain to Barbara that her opinion of the fairer sex was sadly lacking in any form of Christian charity. He went on to point out that just because a young lady was wearing a ludicrously tight skirt combined with stupidly high heels, whose breasts were not only heaving, but also seemingly trying to escape and because not a single one of her hair follicles could remember it's original colour, did not mean she was a "porn star" or "strumpet" as Barbara had so elegantly described her.

"What about the eyelashes?"

"Stupid."

"So you wouldn't have."

"Didn't say that, she might be nice, got to give everyone a chance."

"Bloody men, I'm saving you from yourself here, you should thank me, you'd just make a fool of yourself."

"I thought you had seen my band."

"Good point."

"Is this practise for the beach?" Barbara had been holding Andy's hand since dragging him away from his inevitable humiliation. "Only it's not midnight and this aint a beach." She let go and they stood out side the gothic drinking emporium. The flame lamps lit the street and through the windows one could see the vague shadows of happy Goths sitting in the throne chairs, supping their blood red cocktails as they pretended to like the music. Barbara pulled him back from the door and started to explain.

"On the fateful night two years ago, I came wandering up here, and you should have seen me, I'd had my hair done, nails done, new shoes, dress, everything. I'd been plucked and scrubbed and buffed and polished, and some waxing, ow, all for you."

"Tell me about the hair; was it big?"

"It had it's own ozone lair, Nasa were planning missions."

"The shoes?"

"Oh still got them, very silly, but never mind that, do you want to know or what?"

"Ok, carry on."

"So, there I was, the most glamorous girlie ever, the most beautiful girl you'd ever seen."

"Always were."

"Shut up." Barbara took his hand and led him in. "I was out there and you were sitting here, on one of these, this one will do, sit down. So you were here and I was there and you had some blonde woman all over you and you had her enormous tits in your hands and I just thought, "fuck you" and went home."

"That was Mandy, idiot boy was right next to me, that was the first time she'd been out with her weapons of mass destruction."

"Well I know that now, but at the time. God, I'd spent ages getting ready, you know the whole human Barbie thing takes time and it can be painful, in fact it fucking hurts, ever been waxed? Look it had been my last day, I'd just changed jobs, I was in an absolutely foul mood and have I mentioned the pain? You get your fucking legs waxed, it's not a joyous experience, and I'd decided that I was gong to shag your brains out, eat you alive, just filth and there you were playing with some slags tits, you should have been playing with mine, so I went home. Sorry. Two of them please." Barbara pointed to the top of a list and the lady behind the bar brought two test tubes full of red stuff.

"Right; go! Two more please."

"Tell me about the shoes."

"I fucking hated you, oh red and shiny, very slutty."

"And you have still got them."

"Suppose you want to see them?"

"I'm quite prepared to beg."

"Oh for god's sake, two more please."

"So, again so, if I hadn't been playing with two bin bags full of luke warm custard all those years ago?"

"Just as a matter of interest, did you enjoy it?"

"Not really."

"Not really, what does that mean?"

"Well I can see a use for them."

"Oh stop, enough, don't want to know."

"Back to the point; It's two years ago and I'm here on my own, with my new shirt on, did I mention that? Well there I am waiting for you, a vision of loveliness, a goddess, a super model, an angel a…"

"I was more; big haired slut, but never mind, it was more like this." Barbara pulled off her srunchy and threw her hair forward, ran her fingers through it, licked her lips and repeated, "More like this."

"Oh I'm in love."

"Then I would probably have given you a little kiss like this and a bit of a hug, just holding on a little bit too long and then I would have realised

that you were way to scruffy for me and gone of
with some blonde Adonis."

"It's a Goth pub, you don't get blonde Adonis's in
places like this, and you would have broken my
heart anyway."

"I did not break your heart."

"You fucking did. Do we have to dwell on this?"

"No, get a couple of pints, I'm going for a wiz, I'll
see you down stairs."

Down stairs in the Pit made the darkness upstairs
seem positively radiant. Andy did as bid and found
an alcove in the darkness, an alcove for two.

"Wow!"

"I've brushed my hair, it's no big deal."

"Anyway as I was saying, it will probably take me
a lifetime to collect the shards of my broken heart
and piece them together so I can ever love again."

"Full of shit, you don't even like girls like me, you
like little bimbo sluts, Mandy's friend, that sort of
thing, the one I saved you from."

"Ah you see that's where you are wrong, girls like
that are just a poor substitute for the real thing,
stroppy ginger haired heart breakers like you."

"It's fucking auburn."

"Whatever, never again will I be able to
experience the oneness of being."

"The oneness of being, what kind of shit is that."

"No Idea, look missis you are directly responsible
for the two most erotic experiences of my life, so

far. Haven't ruled out something else cropping up
at some point, but so far.."

"We never did anything!"

"You kissed me, tongues and everything."

"That was not erotic."

"Made me lumpy, and the other, the other remains
my final stroke fantasy."

"Final stroke fantasy! you perv."

"The shoe shop, ahh, the shoe shop."

"I needed shoes for a wedding."

"Thirteen pairs!"

"Possibly not."

"You tried on thirteen pairs of high heels and
danced around the shop asking me if they were too
slutty, then you put a pair in my lap and made me
do up all the little straps, such a tart."

"And that's the most filthy and erotic thing that's
ever happened to you?"

"Erotic; yes. Filthy, no."

"Tell me the filthy stuff."

"No!"

"Go on."

"No and I do not want to know what you have
been getting up to with your married man."

"I'm getting rid."

"Sure you are."

"Really I am."

"Look if you are scared of having no one pencilled
in for when ever, pencil in ANDY, I'd rather you

did it with an indelible marker but a pencil would be good enough, for now."

"I don't need someone to pencil in. I like time to myself, got loads to do."

"Me too, going to paint and draw all summer, got it all planned. Don't need anyone getting in the way."

"That's alright then, what are the paintings like?"

"Brilliant!"

"Ha, ha."

"Well they are, I'm not pissing about here, it's all good stuff."

"When do I get to see them?"

"Any time you like, I've got fourteen done and need to have thirty two by September."

"Why?"

"Exhibition, don't look so shocked, I'm having an exhibition, just haven't done all the work yet. What have you got planned?"

"I'm moving." A face fell.

"A whole four miles away." A face recomposed.

"Would you like a hand? Or has Mr. Fuckhead got it all under control."

"Mr. Fuckhead knows bugger all about it, and yes I'd love a hand."

"Will it involve lifting heavy boxes?"

"Oh yes, trying to wimp out now?"

"No just want to be straight on the level of recompense."

"I'll purchase for you a pint of your chosen poison.
Don't look at me like that, I'm not shagging you
just coz you helped me lift some boxes, fucking
hell."

"You are so heartless."

"I'll learn to live with it, is the offer still open?
Good. I'm getting the boxes tomorrow, pack them
up on Sunday, ready to go on Tuesday, Janice is
going to help, it'll take a few journeys, but we can
handle it. I've got a two day cross over, so there's
no rush, sort of planned it."

"I know a man with a van."

"Yes I'm sure you do, probably expect me to sleep
with him as well."

"No just me, but he will want to see the video."

"Oh piss off back to the party; I'm sure your little
porn dolly is pining for you."

"Don't want her, ooh that sounded rather petulant,
did it not?"

"Yes. Do you really know a man with a van."

"Mmm, I'm sure if you bung him a few quid he
will be willing, one thing, he's got a real job so it
would have to be in the evening."

"Real job?"

"Not a teacher."

"You know some one who isn't a teacher, I'm sure
there is some law against that."

"There bloody well should be, can't have any of
them there subversive ideas getting through, don't
these people realise how important a Btec is?"

"A step too far, shall we go back or do you want another one here?"

"If we return I will have to play the guitar and you will not be able to contain your self, pants will fly, sorry knickers."

"Best stay here then, go on, your turn." Andy did as bid and went to the bar as Led Zeppelin went off to Kashmir; some things never change.

Barbara took a sip from her fresh pint, checked her mobile and passed it across.

"We are being summoned."

"Oh dear, she's not a happy bunny."

Andy took his own chunk of now retro technology from his pocket, slid open the lid and started to check his messages when it rang.

"What?"

"Thought you were going to play, where are you?"

"I've been kidnapped."

"Rubbish."

"Seriously, this ginger, sorry auburn babe has led me astray, abducted me and wishes to have her evil way, for gods sake do not pay the ransom!" Andy pressed the off switch and returned the little piece of star trek to his pocket.

"Suppose we should go back."

"But not yet." Barbara picked up her pint.

A single eyebrow was raised as its owner saw, from the vantage of the upstairs function room window, Andy and Barbara walking hand in hand as they entered the pub below. When Janice joined them they were seated on the high stools by the bar. As she stood before them, talking biscuits, Andy rolled up Barbara's sleeve, kissed her shoulder and rolled it back down. Janice continued wittering on for a full forty five seconds before the realisation of what she had just seen sunk in.

"What did you just do?"

Barbara turned and looked at him.

"Yes, what the fuck was that?"

"That madam was a physical manifestation of my adoration of, not just your shoulder or even your entire arm but absolutely everything attached to it. Or them, I'm a bit lost now, but do not fret my good lady I do not just mean the all too obvious charms contained within your magnificent feminine physic but also the brain and it's fearsome intellect."

"Oh, that's alright then."

"No it bloody isn't, I've never heard so much crap in my life, well no that's not strictly true, but come on Barbara, what pile of doo doo."

"I'll do it again if you want."

"Maybe later."

"Where the fuck have you been, come on mate you are on." A very relived Pete led our hero (for that is what he is, just in case you were wondering when the hero would turn up) away to spank the plank.

"What the hell are you playing at?"

"Janice, I have no idea, but it was quite nice, let's go and watch him make a twat of himself."

"What about all your; never look back, always go forwards speech you always give me, what about all that crap?"

"You're getting a bit previous, come on he's just a guy I knew years ago, nothing ever happened."

"Yes but you wanted to."

"Well now I might."

"Might?"

"Oh look at your sweaty drummer, my god he's a wet as you, god woman I can smell it."

"Enough."

"Deeply deranged."

Andy handed back the red guitar the second he realised they were indeed going to play the entire three years of " Freebird." Enough was enough.

"Barbara sweetie shall we beat a hasty retreat to the downstairs hostelry, this is going to be nine minutes we wont get back, come let us adjourn below before this bird has time to change." Barbara picked up her jacket and bag, told Andy that he really was full of shit and left Janice drooling at the sight of the sweaty drummer.

"This has got to be the last drink; I'm just not used to this anymore."

"Such a liar."

"No; seriously, not used to it these days."

"The trick is not to have the last one, that's the one that does it, makes you do the stupid stuff, gives you the hangover. I've done extensive research into this."

"So if the next one is the last one and we don't have it, all will be well."

"That's about the size of it."

"Good plan."

Half way through the not the last drink, drink, Barbara decided she needed to see the paintings and she didn't care how messy things were chez Andrew. Then there was the neck rub, and then the little argument and then the search for condoms.

"You are a bloke, you are meant to have them."

"I was not expecting this situation to arise."

"Is that you being funny, or attempting."

"Yeah."

"Oh dear, have you really not got any? What if you had brought the little porn dolly back, bet you could find one for her."

"I was never going to bring her back, I haven't brought anyone home for ages."

"Obviously, the place is a tip and when did you last change the sheets?"

"Wednesday, two days ago, and it's only the front room that's a tip and I did warn you."

"Suppose you can't turn the clock back."

"I'm not trying to turn the clock back."

"So what are we playing at?"

"For fucks sake, I met a stunning woman at a party I didn't even want to go to, she took all her clothes off and got into my bed, it would have been rude to try and stop her."

"Oh so now I'm a slut."

"I did not say that."

"I did, come on; here's me at a party, I meet some bloke, fall for his "Do you want to see my etchings" bollox and end up in his bed with no knickers on desperately searching for out of date condoms, Jesus what a floozie."

"Good point."

"This is my life; an affair with a married man and jumping into bed with some failed rock star, I thought it would be more substantial by now."

"Substantial?"

"Oh I don't know."

"Are you coming back to bed?"

Barbara had been walking round the edge of the futon for the past ten minutes.

"In a minute, Andy do you think we would have had, you know, midnight walks along moonlight beaches, all that crap that other people do, the nice stuff, you know."

"Certainly, may have been a little argument along the way."

"Can I have a cuddle?"

"Come here, and try not to stand on me again."

"Andy, can I have my two years back?"

"I shall wave my magic wand."

"I could make a highly inappropriate joke here."
"Good because, to the untrained eye, this could be misconstrued as an almost genuinely tender moment."
"Cynicism at this time of night, that's a gift. I do like your paintings."
"Sarcasm at this time of night, that too is a gift."
"Oh shut up, go to sleep."

A full minute and a quarter passed before Barbara broke the saggy elastic tension of silence.
"You are going to have such sore balls in the morning."
"I know."
"I'd help you out but I don't want to be painted as a slut, a cheap floozie or a lady of dubious morals."
"I would never entertain such an idea, oh."
Barbara let go.
"No, it's just not right."
"Seriously I'd think you were simply wonderful."
"Sorry I just can't." She stroked him some more, "I'd just feel so cheap."
"Feeling cheap can be a good thing."
"Oh these are going to hurt like hell tomorrow."
"Oh, god, please, that's not fair."
"Sorry Andy, I just can't, if I did this." She did, "It would only be one step away from this." Barbara took Andy's thumb and proceeded to be decidedly un- ladylike about it." She removed it. "Except not with your finger."

"That was a thumb."

"Whatever, it's just not right."

"Barbara, is it raining?"

"That's disgusting, stop licking your fingers, you should be ashamed, where are you going? Oh dear, I'm such a slut!"

How they ended up looking at each other's feet was anyone's guess.

"What's the time?"

Andy found his mobile.

"Nearly four."

"Oh god I've got to get some kip, loads to do tomorrow, or today.

"Perhaps if you shut up the winged angel of nocturnal bliss would pass over you."

"The winged angel of nocturnal bliss! What?"

"Yes, that's the chap, sweeps across and touches you little nose and drops you off in sleepy land."

"What?"

"Or you could just shut up and we could go to sleep."

Andy hauled himself up the bed and lay next to her.

"Oh this is weird; I haven't woken up next to anyone for ages."

"That's because you're an insomniac."

"No it's coz he always goes home, he has got a wife you know."

"Yeah thanks for reminding me about that, and the winged angel of nocturnal bliss tickles you cute nose and you drift off into a blissful slumber."

"That was your finger."

"Night. Night."

Chapter two

In which the walk of shame is avoided and some flat pack boxes are assembled, sounds like an exciting chapter to me.

"Walk of shame then?"
"And a good morning to you milady, I thought you wanted a hand, boxes or something. I am willing to help, or are you just too, too ashamed?"
"No I want my two years back, what's the time Mr. Wolf?"
Andy handed the alarm clock over.
"Shit, bugger and wank, right if you want to help; we had best get a shift on."

"Come on I'm dying for a wee."
"Well have one, I wont look, honest."
"Sing something, you don't want to hear this."
"I'd better not mention my pee fetish now, yeah, yeah.
I'd better not mention my pee fetish now, yeah, yeah
I'd better not mention my….oh hello."
Barbara stepped into the shower.
"Shift, shampoo, that's not shampoo, that's shower jell. God we need to go shopping."
"Yes dear."

"Oh come on; some shampoo, a bit of conditioner, not much to ask."

Barbara left the shower and started shouting, and on and on...

"Andy can we please get a shift on, oh there you are. Come on, storage place near the County ground, you know it? Good come on."

Barbara jumped out of the car.

"Put the seats up." She ran to the little office and quickly retuned with an arm full of shrink - wrapped flat packed boxes, then more, then more. Some money was exchanged and she was back in the car.

"Can we get a move on please?"

"If you told me where we were going!"

Directions were given, and then some more.

"Shit, she's never on time."

"Who what where why when how, I'm a little lost here."

"I wanted to at least pretend not to be a dirty little stop out."

"Oh, does it matter? Who's going to know? Am I that bad? These and other questions will be.."

"Answered in this weeks episode of "Soap" very good, look; she's a girl and I'm wearing the same clothes."

"How bad can it be?"

"Oh just you wait, it'll be worse if she says nothing, and there she is, shit!"

Boxes were moved; boxes were prefabricated; boxes were filled. Andy was allocated books and Cd's and spent most of the afternoon shouting, "I wondered where that had gone." to no one in particular.

By six fifteen there were seventeen boits of assorted stuff piled up in Barbara's front room. By six fifty five they were eating pizza and assorted sundries.

"Barbara, you must have had those knickers on for at least twenty hours, aren't they getting a bit smelly."

"You said she'd be funny."

"I was wrong, anyway Janice; did you get your claws into that sweaty drummer bloke?"

Janice shook her head in a "We are not all sluts" manner.

"What, Norman. I'll phone him for you." Andy flipped his phone and made the appropriate actions.

"Normy Normal, how you? Look I've got some girl here; she's lusting after you, big time. She saw you playing last night and wants your babies, or to lick the sweat off your bum or something. Can you remember her? Big tits, pretty, slim; Would I? Can't say at this present moment in time, here, talk to her." A phone was passed over to an aghast Janice.

"Hello….. there's no one there, you sod!"

"I'm not that mean, but that's his number, oh and by the by Barbara; he's the man with the van."

"The man with the van you say."

"Indeed, just get Janice to shag him and he'd probably do it for half price or something, ow, bugger."

"You can be such a twat, I'd forgotten about that."

"Soz!"

The small piece of pizza had been thrown with considerable force. Barbara pulled it off and ate it.

"Yuk!"

"Are you calling him or not?"

Janice passed the phone back.

"No."

"I will." Barbara took the phone and pressed the button.

"Hi, is that Norman? Good, your mate."

"That would be Andy then."

"How did you know?"

"You are on his phone."

"Oh yeah, duh. Well he says you have a van and as I'm moving house; I could do with a man with a van. No it's not far, probably take about an hour, could you? Brilliant, Tuesday evening, six thirty it is, fifty quid alright?" Barbara gave her current and intended address and handed the phone back to its owner who looked at the pile.

"It should all fit, it would all fit if you took all the crap out; yes I'll give you a hand. Oh and her mate wants to shag you, see ya."

"No I dont." Janice kept on hitting him.

"Janice, he's a bloke, we don't do subtle."

"I'll have to face him now, what am I going to say?"

"You don't have to say anything, just do your hair flicky thing and smile."

"What hair flicky thing?"

"That hair flicky thing."

"Is that all it takes?"

"Considerably less, everything up to the kick in the balls is good, men are stupid, I should know."

"That's just you."

"Cheers Barb."

"Don't call me Barb."

"He's just a walking pizza now."

"Barbara; your mad friend is licking my face."

"It's the last bit and I'm hungry." Janice peeled the last slice from Andy's nose but decided, upon reflection, not to eat it. Snot as an optional extra had never been the top of her list.

Then it was the morning after, Janice had gone. There had been some shopping, some talking, a lot of peaceful quiet, some arguing (of the; he was never in Star Trek, variety) some sweating, a little grunting, some oohs and aahs and far too much giggling, but precious little sleep.

"What one would you want?"

Barbara showed him two saved texts; one a diatribe of venomous vitriol outlining each and every single one of his failings, the other a simple statement of facts.

"It's over; bye."

Andy read them both and despite various misgivings and reinforced preconceptions opted for option number two. Barbara pressed send.

"That's that then."

"What?"

"Not you, bloody hell, I've just waved bye byes to the last year of my life, a weight has been lifted. I feel good, dad a dad a dad a da, I knew that I would now."

"Please stop singing."

Barbara threw her arms round his neck and started dragging his sorry carcass in time to her very own little song, she felt good, and she knew that she would.

The lunch was in the way of a thank you for all your help but soon degenerated into an afternoon of utter debauchery, followed but some disastrous attempts at box opening, one box anyway.

"I can't go on drinking like this, and our diet's been appalling."

"It's fine for a few days but I wouldn't want to get used to it."

"Thought it was all sex and drugs and rock and roll for you."

"Rock and roll and driving everywhere, no sex or drugs for me."

"Poor thing."

"Hardly Led Zep, and speaking of which tell your crazy face licking mate her delicious drummer is playing with us tomorrow."

"Deserting me in my hour of need already, I thought you cared, but no; you just cast me aside for a cheap red guitar."

"It's white and it was two hundred and forty nine pounds."

"Like I said, cheap! I thought you had a red Strat."

"Well yes but I'm using a white one at the moment."

"Ooh, get you, what time?"

"Usual till late."

"I'll bring her along."

Around about and pretty close to half an hour after the hour after the hour that had been mentioned the pair arrived in style. Janice had rock chick-ed it up to the point of self parody and Barbara had found her old leather jacket, they were also both at least four or five inches taller than usual and as they teetered around were on the receiving end of many a rum comment from the grunting baboons in attendance. The old tourist joke still applied. Bars like this were not used to unaccompanied members on the fairer side of the gender divide, not this gorgeous anyway. Bars like this catered for the delusional middle-aged bloke who still thought he could make it big if he just got the right break. The predominantly male reservation was torn asunder by Barbara's "Oh fuck off you sad fat wanker" approach. Members of the lesser species fell by the wayside. She had developed this manner over the years and it never really failed. Didn't make many friends though. The beery mobs inference of her oh so subtle handing the pint to the lead guitarist clicked in. You could almost hear the cogs turning. "Oh she's with him, why's it always the lead guitarist, bastard." All her immaculately constructed femininity fell away and she was now one of them. Attention shifted to Janice, she had not been spoken for but with a little point of her pointy pink nail in the direction of the drummer she too was accepted by the maddened throng, all twelve of them. Whilst waiting at the bar for the endless song to finally die, Janice and Barbara were accosted by strange men who began to tell them how good their other half's were, how they had long been their favourite local musos, men are strange like this, they just are.

Andy handed his guitar to a very fat bloke and jumped off the stage. It was only a foot and a half high so didn't exactly qualify as stage diving.

"Hey look, rock chicks, real live rock chicks, cool boots. Oh shit not this, please, and in an American accent. Jesus wept. I used to like this song."

"I still do."

"Oh Janice…good grief, look the thing is, this song, this bloody song, and this is only my over opinionated point of view, but, this song comes in and out of ones life like a viral tax collector. Just when you think it's safe it comes on the radio or something, and there you have it, by the time it's over you remember why you hated it in the first place. Ok the bit where the guitar solo kicks in is perhaps one of the finest moments in recorded music history, but it's downhill from there."

"Confusing your own opinion with fact again."

"Tell you what, once you have heard fat boy here mangle it into submission, you, even you, will never, ever, ever want to hear it again."

"Is he the poster boy for weight watchers?"

"Meanie."

"I am going off it."

"Told you, there is only one correct place for this song and that's in the wee small hours and only if you are drunk as a skunk, then and only then is it appropriate to play it over and over on the DVD till you pass out."

"And she's buying…oh I've gone right off it."

"Don't worry Janice, he's got some very bizarre theories about music, which he will go on and on about until you hit him on the arm. Andy please, please explain to me how brilliant Cheap Trick are again."

"If I had been talking utter bollox you would not have remembered."

"You played "The Flame" in the car all the time."

"Rubbish."

"For a week, everyday for a week, not just once, but over and over. Jesus. Oh just once more."

"I like that one."

"Not for a week. And what about "These boots are made for walking." That was one of yours."

"That bloody Shania Twain cd."

"That was your's."

"Bollox, I put it in one of your boxes yesterday."

"Only coz I stole it from you, not because I liked it, just to stop you playing it!"

"Excuse me, are you like this all the time?"

"Like what?" They both looked at her.

"At least we don't lick pizza off strangers faces."

"Don't get much stranger than him. Oh here he comes, remember; hair flicky and big smile, watch this, she's been practicing. Olympic standard, and they are under starters orders and away they go..."

"Oh very good; ten out of ten for content, another ten for style and fifteen for perceived intent, wow! Your friends a bit much."

"Hi, Normy Normal."

"Hi, What? I know you from somewhere. Oh I remember, that was a while ago."

"Ten out of ten for bluffing, it's like it never happened."

"Oh it happened, Barbara, how did I remember that. Oh yeah he never shut up about you, even when he was shagging the blonde."

"Thanks Norm."

"Oops."

"Tell me about the blonde."

"I just made her up, anyway who's moving, coz if it's you, sorry I don't know your name, I'm Norman, drummer to the stars, well mostly idiot boy here, but anyway if you do that hair flicky thing again I'll move anything you like anywhere you want."

Janice started flicking her hair from side to side and making little girlie faces.

"You mean this shit really works."

"God yes, men are crap, I mean look at him, and he just pretends to be a man, on the other had I…"

"Used to be a woman called Hilda."

"How did you know?"

"It was in the Daily Mail. Sorry to shatter your illusion but it's me that wants to use your van, I'm sure Janice could find you something dainty and cute to pick up afterwards."

"Yes, well whatever, I do remember you, you came to one gig and took pictures, your hair was redder."

"It's auburn!"

"And a very lovely shade too. So Janice.." Andy and Barbara were cut out with laser precision.

"This cute dainty thing."

"Well, it might make you sweat."

"Oh for fucks sake." Barbara grabbed Andy's hand and dragged him off. "Come on, I'll help you with your guitar packing away stuff."

"No you wont."

"I'll watch."

"No you wont."

"Probably right, oh look, she is terrible, you have no idea how bad she is, one time at a party, she knew I could see her, god! She did her little hair flicky thing and… I can't tell you, but she knew I was watching, I couldn't believe it. She looks so sweet."

"She looks like Elvira."

"Go and get your stuff."

Barbara wandered off and spoke to many people about things she knew nothing about. It's what Barbaras do.

"Is she going to be ok with him?"

"Is he going to be ok with her? Can we stay here tonight?" She took two packages from her bag and put them on the table. One contained shampoo. "Only it would be the last night in my wee house and I don't want a last night, I'd just cry all night. So if last night was the last night then, does this make sense?"

"Sort of."

Barbara's phone made its special ring tone noise.

"Oh yes, sure, mm. So he dropped you off and you had a little kissy and you're seeing him tomorrow.

Such a liar, I bet you have him tied to the bed already. Janice I can hear him grunting in the back ground, that's never the fridge, well perhaps, yes I'm sure he likes you; now take his cock out of your mouth and put the phone down, goodnight."
 Barbara stretched out on the couch and put her feet in his lap. He started undoing the laces.
"This could take some time."
"Mmmm." Barbara wiggled her feet again.

 The move went remarkably smoothly, nothing got lost and after Janice had whisked Norman away to do some "Heavy Lifting" Barbara and Andy managed to christen most of the house in a conjoined manner, even the upstairs and the stairs.

 The following day the new occupiers of Barbara's old abode awoke happy and secure in their new home. It was only when their nine year old daughter asked her mother what a whore was that they realised that something may be amiss. Across the window and front door in neon green spray paint the words "You fucking whore" had mysteriously appeared. This, it would transpire was not a neighbourhood welcoming committee tradition regularly imposed on new families, nor was it a teenage prank. The police were called; Barbara was called.
 "Not off hand, I'll come round." She covered the mouthpiece with her hand and called Andy over to

listen in. "Of course you can give my number to the police, have you got a crime number yet? Good I'll call them, Give us half and hour and we'll be there." She replaced the phone. "Idiot boy has really done it now."

"I thought I was idiot boy?"

"No you're...." She stopped to think. "You're; Mister Hunky take me now, woof, woof."

"Funny that, last night I distinctly remember being called "Idiot Boy""

"That was last night when you were being an idiot."

"Wandering around with you wrapped around my waist working out if we'd done it in here yet."

"All you had to do was remember, my god is it that difficult, and we still have one left."

"You can carry me this time."

"Wuss."

Barbara drove back down her lonesome road; she hadn't expected to be doing this route again so she took Andy with her. It all seemed a bit strange but not as strange as the violent green slanderous graffiti. Andy pointed out that it changed colours depending on the viewpoint and this meant that it wasn't cheap paint.

"Oh yes, hey that's cool, don't suppose this has anything to do with you? You haven't got a mad ex who's taken a dislike to me? Some clingy bint who just cant let go?" Barbara proceeded to get awfully am dram, clinging to his arm and wiping her fevered brow. The hair tossing was good.

"Not that I know of."

"Oh you are so cruel, you can't even remember all the little hearts you have broken."

"I didn't mean it like that, No there is no demented bint from my despicable past chasing after you just coz you've run away with me."

"Run away with…"

"Sounds like fun to me, we could go to Birmingham."

"Birmingham!"

"Tres chic."

"No it's not, anyway it's probably not idiot boy, he's not that stupid, and he's on holiday, and he's old enough to know better."

"What about his wife?"

"Never met the woman, well actually I have but we're not going into that."

"Oh yes we are, come on let's delve."

"Later, I'll tell you everything."

"No you wont."

"Too right, oh whose knocking, you'll have to do it, too weird for me."

"So why not Mrs. Dick Face Mc Poodle pants then? Why couldn't she do this?"

"Way too cool, he'd just wake up dead and she'd be the perfect grieving and very wealthy widow. I only met her once; quite liked her."

"And there you were shagging her husband, oh hello."

A little girl with a long blonde ponytail had opened the door,

"Are you the whore?" She paused for a moment, twisted her head round the doorframe, looked at the front of her new house and continued. "The fucking whore?"

"I'm not, but she might be." Andy pointed at Barbara.

"Mum, the fucking whore is here."

"Clarrisa! We have asked you to mind your language, Hi Barbara, any idea what's going on."

"Not a sausage." Andy was introduced but he was busy showing Clarissa how the paint changed colour as you walked past it. Clarissa soon got bored and asked what exactly "A fucking Whore" was.

"It's not really a good thing, for future reference, doctors, dentists, things like that, they are the good things."

"I'm going to be a whale psychologist, I saw it on telly, you get to swim with whales and wear pink flippers, I just want the pink flippers."

"Sounds cool to me."

Barbara and Clarissa's mum had a slightly embarrassed "are you sure it's not you, oh well it must be me" conversation.

"What did the police have to say?"

The police had been and the police had seen and the police had asked some questions along the lines of "Are you sure it's nothing to do with you?" and the police had allocated a crime scene number and the police had gone away. A community officer had been asked to keep an eye out for any further suspicious behaviour or occurrences but didn't expect much, there being no witnesses or concrete evidence. Clarissa's mum and dad were, it would seem, the perfect couple, no extra marital rumpy pumpy or any hidden secrets, at least not that they could remember.

Barbara offered, or rather offered Andy, to help clear up the mess but it was all in hand. They were going to paint the front of the house and now it would be sooner rather than later. Before they left Barbara had Andy take a picture of her good self standing in front of her accusers graffiti. Perhaps not the equivalent of the old "Clapton is God" complete with weeing mutt but a good souvenir all the same.

"What did it say again?"
"Not nice."
"Go on, what did it say?"
"You know what it said, you have a photo of it."
"Go on, tell me what it said?"
"It's rude."
"Yeah, I know, just say it."
"No."

"Do you think I am?"

"Na, I think your lovely."

"Not a fucking whore then?"

"No!"

"How about a cocksucking slut?"

"Where did that come from?"

"I don't know, go on tell me what it said."

"No!"

"Whisper it in my ear."

"No!"

"Why not?"

"You happen to be driving."

"No fun. I have a feeling someone don't like me."

"It didn't say that, nor did it say shameless hussy, which I'm beginning to think you could well be, a lascivious shameless hussy no less."

"Not a cocksucking whore then?"

"Nope."

"What did it say?"

"It said you were a jolly nice person, perhaps a little over friendly in the physical department."

Barbara's plan had worked and she was now pulling her jeans back on.

"Well that's it then."

"What is?"

"All the rooms."

"Oh yeah, I feel used, I do have feelings you know."

"Bollocks, you're a man."

"You can't just use me as and when you feel like it."

"Why not?"

"It's not the done thing."

"Tis now."

"Tell me what it said."

"Floozie."

"No."

"Fucking whore."

"That's the one."

"Good paint."

"Right, bugger off."

"What?"

"Do you want to help me unpack all this stuff?"

"I'll bugger off."

There was the three thirty call about the lost screwdriver, which was where she'd left it after they had put the bed together. There was the four seventeen call about the missing box of cd's that wasn't missing at all. There was the four thirty call apologising for the four seventeen call. There was the six o'clock call, just coz she felt like it. There was the eight thirty call about putting the bookcase together. There was the nine thirty call about boredom and wanting a drink. Andy put the painting in his trusty old Clio and set off for a night of adventure.

"When did you do this? It's still wet!"

"You don't have to have it."

"What is it?"

"An orange tree."

"It's got bananas on it."

"It's an orange tree with extra bits."

" So I get to keep it."

"That's the general idea."

"Mmm."

"You can take it down when your friends come round."

"Or just put it up when you're here."

"That would cover it."

And then someone's tongue was in someone else's mouth and there was oodles of tenderness and no one was called a fucking whore. Then a bookcase was reassembled and then the phone rang.

There had been an arson attack at Barbara's old house. The family had got out but Clarissa'a dad had been badly burned rescuing his daughter. The police seemed to think someone shoving fire works through the letterbox had started it. They wanted to know if Barbara could shed any light on the situation. After all someone did seem to hold a grudge against her.

"Andy, I don't want to tell the boys in blue about my stupid little affair, anyway it's not him, or her, they are on holiday in France, and I really cant see him or her paying someone to do this. What do I tell them? Are you sure it's got nothing to do with you? Everyone has a psycho ex somewhere."

"Loads of them but how could they know about you?"

"Loads of them?"

"Na, not really. The last one dumped me, she's not going to care what I'm doing now."

"Or who."

"Oh ha, ha aren't we the funny one."

"Well yes actually I am."

"What you going to say to plod then?"

"The truth, I haven't got a clue what's going on."

Some of the answers were delivered with the mornings post. Along with some legal bumf, some junk, a bunch of menus and a huge advert for DFS, was some stuff bundled together and sent on from Barbara's ex and now burnt residence. Barbara went from "Ooh this looks exciting" to "Shit!" in a matter of seconds. The first envelope opened contained a "Never mind the bollocks" style note. The cinematic newspaper cut out read as a warning. "Leave him alone you bitch!"

"Well that's subtle, the wife?"

"On holiday in France, look at the post mark, it's local and only a few days ago."

"What is it you are not telling me? There's got to be something."

Barbara was turning pale.

"What is it you are not showing me?"

Barbara folded the paper in two.

"Oh shit, look there is probably something I should tell you, given the circumstances and all that. But before I do, oh bollox, look, this last couple of days, well you know, I actually like you, you know a lot, god I'm starting to sound like some nut job bunny boiler."

"How bad does this get?"

"Oh fuck." She handed him one of the sheets.

It was a picture, a picture of her. A very flattering picture of her; a somewhat compromising picture of her, dressed as a school girl, a porno school girl, hair in bunches, high heels, stockings, usual stuff. But she wasn't alone. She was bent over the knee of the man who was administering the spanking.

"Oh dear, who's been a naughty girl then." He looked at her. She looked back, pulled her hair into bunches and made a cute face.

"Look Andy it gets worse, we made films and stuff, I got a copy, he got a copy, no one else was ever going to see it."

"Let me see it."

"It gets bad, really bad."

"Ok I don't want to see it, but it seems someone else has, this is a screen grab. How many of these tings did you do?"

"There's hours of it, oh for god's sake it was fun, we'd just think up bizarre shit and film it, just for us, no one was going to see it, just for fun, I wasn't coerced or anything, half of it was my idea. I'm going to fucking kill him. Ok so I am a fucking whore and you never want to see me again, don't blame you."

"I didn't say that, don't be silly, not keen on the school girl thing, but I'll make films with you if you want, sounds like fun to me."

"I'm never doing this again, no way. You don't mind about this stuff?"

"Not too keen on finding out my new girlfriend is a porn star, but, is it on the Internet? Oh dear."

"Oh fuck, don't say that, oh god. I'm not a bloody porn star, two of us and a camera, that's not porn."

"Kinda looks like it to me. You do look good."
Barbara looked at the picture.

"Yes I do, but that's not the point."

"Have you still got those shoes?"

"Yes, I've got all of it, somewhere and that's not the point either. Someone else has got hold of this stuff. For all I know this could already be on the Internet. Oh god! Andy this is awful I'm fucked here, well here to be precise." She showed him another picture.

"I don't want to see that, well I sort of do, you do look good, love the hair. You know what makes it worse is I kind of know him."

"Yes that's worse, how the hell do you know him?"

"He comes to the jam, not every week, usually got some cute little blonde with him, don't think it's his wife and it's certainly not his daughter."

"No, she's got dark hair and his daughter is about twelve or something, good god does the man ever stop, bastard. Should I tell the police about this?"

"Tell them about your little affair and show the sex pistols thing but I wouldn't show them any of these, hang on that's not you."

"Oh yeah, distinct lack of ginger minge."

"I thought it was auburn."

"Oh yeah, come on lay them out. Me, me, me, oh dear not that one, oh no." Barbara turned a few pictures over. "You sure about this, the me and you thing."

"How much worse does it get?"

"Doesn't get any worse, there's just a lot of it."

"Well I don't have to look, you do look cute though; that's not you." More and more badly printed screen shots were laid out.

"Oh god I know her, she's still at work, had two kids since then. These are ancient."

"She doesn't know the camera's there, I mean you are practically waving at the thing, she hasn't a clue. Who is this guy?"

"I thought you knew him?"

"Only to say hi to, don't know his name or anything, don't know what he does."

"He's the deputy head, don't say a thing, that giggling does not help."

Of the fifteen sheets, most were of Barbara, some of her old friend and a few of a younger girl. Andy recognised the tattoo.

"Hang on I know her, I used to give her a lift. Hair's a different colour now."

"And we all know what happens when you give a girl a lift."

"Yes they go on to make porno with their deputy heads."

"Soufflé, She was a student teacher at our place about a year ago, Rachel or Anne or something."

"That's her, and she doesn't look like she knows she's on camera. Look at the angle, no idea, and it's been taken from an old VHS, look at the tracking bars at the bottom, well on the bottom."

"Oh yes, I wonder if she's had one of these." Barbara picked up the note. "Where's my phone book. God she has changed. You call her."

"What am I going to say?"

"Just ask her if she's had one of these." The letter was rattled again. Andy took out his phone and clicked it into play, before he could do anything the demonic beeps of incoming messages took over. After the thing stopped wobbling he clicked to messages. There were seven from Anne; Anne being the girl with the tattoo on her shoulder.

"Speaking of tattooed devils." Andy handed over his plastic lifeline.

"Andy."; "Andy answer your phone."; "Andy I need to talk to you."; "For fucks sake you tosser, turn your fucking phone on."; "Dick head."; "For fucks sake."; and finally "Please."

"Oh yes, you shagging her or what?"

"No. We don't spend hours in the pub after work, we don't go to films, we don't; whatever we did, I'm afraid it's not like that."

"Why not?"

"Too young."

"Where did you get morals from?"

"Nowt to do with that, she'd wear me out in about three seconds."

"Probably."

"Give me the phone."

"Hello, never mind where I've been or where I am, stop shouting at me, yes I know I'm a wanker. So what the hell is up with you? You have had a letter, oh; it wouldn't be a sort of "Sex Pistols" type thing? What do you mean; who are the Sex Pistols? Is it cut out from a newspaper? Yes, right. Is there a bunch of photographs, well dodgy ones, right, see the one with the school girl, yes the ginger one with the cool shoes, she wants to talk to you." A phone was passed across.

"It's auburn, but they are cool shoes, Hi Anne, I'm Barbara. I knew I was being filmed, I probably pressed the little red button, but you seem to be oblivious. How many pictures have you got, several of me, a few of you and a couple of, yes it is Mary. Has anyone done anything to your house? No, good. Well that's one up on me, look we need to meet up, I'll pass you back to Andy."

"Fucking hell Andy, what am I going to do, what if Jim finds out? What if? What if? Oh shit!"

"Anne, don't say anything to anyone, we'll need to meet up and find out what the hell is gong on. Barbara is trying to get hold of Mary; I'll call you back. Don't say anything to anyone especially Mr. Wonderful."

"Right then, I'm off to the bar, you can plan the murder now, I need plausible deniability."
"Ooh, get you!"
"I did have nice hair then, long time ago, eight years to be precise." Mary put her pictures on the table: three of her, two of Barbara, two of Anne and three of an unknown woman with long dark hair. No one recognised her, or the back ground (but she defiantly knew the camera was there, judging by the smiles and waves) and the pictures were considerably older.
Andy put the drinks down.
"Who's that then? Is she the wife? Are all your pictures the same? These and other questions will be answered in next weeks.."
"Shut up." Barbara handed the picture to him. Anne snatched them back.
"This is bad enough with out monkey boy getting his jollies ooogling these."
"Fair enough, can I see the mystery woman then? I've seen the rest." Three grainy prints were handed over.
"That's not his wife, even ten years ago she wouldn't have looked like that."

"How can you tell it's ten years ago."

"Oh it's probably more, way more, look at the wall paper, the hair, the make up, his comb over!" Mary was quite right; the shag monster definitely had an awesome comb over.

"Is this guy, this bloke here with the super sexy comb over, is he really such an irresistible sex god? Can't see it myself."

"Look Andy, at work he's a charming powerful man."

"Look's like a twat to me."

"Yes but, at work he's.."

"What ever, so he is essentially abusing his position, several of them."

"Not with me he wasn't, I was bored and lonely, it was a right laugh."

"Yes but Barbara, you knew you were being filmed, I didn't."

"So it was abuse of power."

"Definitely abuse with me. Well that's my story and I'm sticking to it."

"Coz I got no reason to lie. Where were these pictures taken, is that his house? Have you ever met him away from his work? He's a tit."

"You don't like him very much."

"I think he's jealous."

"Too right, he's a weasel, I don't get it. Besides what I think doesn't really matter. What matters is getting this stuff back. We need, you need to find out who has got hold of this stuff and perhaps even why. There's some nut job out there with a grudge. If old dangly bollox was putting it about with you three, then there has got to be a few more."

"Thanks, you sure know how to pay a compliment."

"Nice tit's good hair, for fucks sake, look at your self. How many more, and do you really want this stuff in the public realm? There will be a lot more ladies getting these letters, what makes you three so special? That sounded wrong, soz, what makes you three, or rather what connects you lot, other than you were all shagging wonder man here at some point? Has someone got it in for you, the three witches of the apocalypse? I really think that you should track him down and beat shit out of him till he tells you what's going on. You could start with finding out who he's shagging now."

"Andy, you have such a way with words. I admit you do have a point. Barbara when were you?"

"I called it off about, well last mid term. Eight weeks ago, he was none to happy about it. Kept pestering me, said he'd leave his wife, all that shit. Got very upset when I pointed out I had no intention of being a step mum to his three grotty kids. He really lost it."

"How long were you with him? I just want to see if there was a cross over point." Dates were analysed and they came up with a gap of a few months. Andy wondered if there had been an intermediary and after the dirty looks had been cast they all agreed there probably had to have been.

"Probably, well what did you get out of it then?"

"A good reference."

"You would have got that anyway, how did you end it?"

"I was only there for a few months, once I'd gone, well that was it. Out side of work it just felt wrong, inside of work it felt wrong but it was exciting for a while. It just felt creepy after that. How about you."

"This is all a bit Opra."

"Shut up Andy, I was old enough to know better. I'd been on my own for a while and it was all shagging in store cupboards and stuff, loads of fun. Then at his house when his wife was away with the kids; which seemed to be a lot. Then I met Jeff and that was that. He pestered me for a while but once I'd kicked him in the balls he gave up, wish I had that on film."

"None of this has any bearing on the problem in hand, don't make the joke Anne, yes that one, fuck's sake. You have to go to the police, Barbara someone tried to burn your house down."

"What!"

"Oh yes, forgot about that."

"Bloody hell Barbara."

"Well I'd kind of moved, but, yes it was a bit yuk."

"I don't want to show anyone this."

"Not too keen."

Barbara took the tamest picture of herself from the bunch.

"I need to tell the police something, this isn't too bad, well, ooh, oh never mind, you can see his face. I'll keep you lot out but he's being dragged through the mud."

They drank up and decided to keep quiet and see what happened next.

The WPC who interviewed her recognised Barbara's co-star immediately, she tried to hide it but it was no good.

"I'm sorry Miss Case but there is something I need to tell you, this chap, your..emm." WPC Constance Strong pointed. " Him, well he's my old geography teacher."

"Oh dear." Barbara was overcome by a fit of the giggles; then they both started.

"I have no idea who has got hold off this stuff but I'm not to thrilled at the prospect of it being broadcast to all and sundry, it does not seem to be any kind of blackmail situation, well not yet and as for him." It was Barbara's turn to point. "I have left him well and truly alone."

"I assume you don't think he has anything to do with all this?" More pointing in the general direction of the picture and the note ensued. "About who did this, who has access to his files, to his very private files. I also assume you have chummies address. I could go and have a look, see if there has been a break in or whatever."

"Oh you would know, more security than, well, a very secure person indeed."

"I'll give it a check anyway, this I shall leave with you." She handed the small pile back to Barbara. "The less people that see it the better, here's my little card, just in case, you know any more of this comes your way."

"You will be the first to know."

"I doubt that very much, but; make me one of the first."

Time to text..her fingers danced "deep shit going on here call me asap."

Barbara's vibrating reply came just as Andy launched into his last guitar solo of the night. She stepped out into the rain to answer.

"Just shut up and listen, oh hang on." Barbara opened Andy's car and jumped in. "Roger, just listen, just fucking listen, remember our little movies, yes I thought you might, well old bean some bugger has got a hold of them, and I am not too chuffed, oh and remember that cute little student teacher; she's none to pleased with you either, you could have told her she was being filmed. Yes Anne, that's the one. Oh and Mary, yes Mary you could have told her about the camera. Oh yes and who is the dark haired girl? At least she knew she was on camera. What do you mean what dark haired girl; surely you mean which dark haired girl? One of the many, Roger what the fuck is going on."

"Oh shit!" Said the disembodied voice from across the channel.

"Shit indeed, you stupid sod. Who has got access to this stuff? Obviously that's just bollox coz someone has, and just how much of this stuff have you got? I knew you were a dirty perv but this is ridiculous, if any of this gets onto the internet I will rip your gonads off, make you eat them then, and only then, kill you. I mean it; what the fuck is going on, oh yes and someone tried to burn my house down."

"Shit."

"I had moved, not so good for the new residents."

"Barbara you need to check some stuff for me."

"I need to do fuck all for you, you cunt!"

"Barbara, please, you need to check the files."

Evidently there was a spare back door key under the third pot on the left in the green house but you had to get to the burglar alarm under the stairs within ninety seconds and feed in the secret code. One, two, three, four.

"There's a key in the green house and it's; one, two, three, four. You are so crap, what happened to, oh bollox, you are such a twat!"

Barbara could remember where his little office was, the DVD's were in the Frank Zappa section of the cd rack, in the Frank Zappa boxes.

"Oh and Roger the police are involved and one of them recognised you, yes I did show them a picture, Scared the poor girl for life I should imagine, Constance Strong, WPC Constance Strong, you used to teach her, geography to be exact."

"Oh shit!"

"Oh shit does not even come close. We will check your house first thing in the morning, no I'm not bloody doing it now and who "we are" is fuck all to do with you. I will text you and you can call back at your earliest convenience. Enjoy the rest of your holls, good night." Then there was the packing up and the witnessing of Janice taking over Normans life, he seemed to be enjoying it, then they went home and did stuff that young people do when they go home; had some toast, watched a film and got very little sleep.

Chapter three

In which our heroes go house hunting.

The key was where he said it would be, the alarm number worked but there were no Zappa Cds. A text was sent and within two minutes a call received.

"No Zappa, that's what I said, Ok, try Genesis, for fucks sake no one needs this many Genesis Cds, Jesus ok "Trick Of The tail" That is the only good one, oh but look when you open the box it's not "Gone were the dreams he had known as a child.." it's "Elaine, 1986-1991 disc 1" so "Wind and Wuthering" that would be disc two and of course "And then there was three" that would be disc three, god you are a dirty old sod, come on Roger, who knows about this stuff?" Barbara handed the three discs to Andy who had already booted up his laptop, he took them and fed disc one into the side of the machine.

"Are all these just films of your knock offs? Genesis, Captain Beefheart and the missing Zappa, all the stuff your wife really loves. But who knew about the Zappa thing? Some bugger did and they got some stuff with me on it, not the happiest bunny in the world here Rog." Andy was scanning folders and doing silent impressions of an unhappy bunny. "Come off it you tit, someone knows. What about the desk, yes I remember and if you mention any of that ever again I will kill you, understand, good. Under the desk there are two external hard drives and a bin, what do you mean; thank fuck for that? Who has access to the house, other than your immediate bunch of deluded drains on your meagre income? Oh there's the door, I have no idea; I haven't got there yet." Barbara opened the door. "Hello" She recognised the woman straight off.

"And what do you think you are doing here, this is not your house, I am going to call the police." She waggled her mobile in Barbara's face. Barbara handed her own phone over.

"Yes she has red hair and yes she has just said auburn and Roger I really need to speak to you, urgent, like right fucking now or sooner."

"Can I have my phone back?"

"Roger, you call me or I'm digging out the videos and giving them to your wife, I can't believe you have done this you bastard."

Barbara got her phone back.

"I'll call you back, and she's right, you are a bastard." She turned to the mystery neighbour. "Come in."

"Hello Elaine, I think you should have these." Andy handed her the three DVDs.

"Oh." And with that she sat down. "Shit, poo, and buggery, ooh that was a bit anal."

"Have you had some strange mail recently?"

"Oh god, you are the school girl, at least you knew the camera was there."

"So did you."

"Andy!"

"It's alright, he told me he'd got rid of the tapes, even handed me a bag full off broken video bits, and I believed him. I've still got my copies, no video player but the tapes are still in the loft. So long ago, god it went on for years. I do not want my husband to find out now, at the time I would not have been all that concerned but now, well things change. Have you any idea what is going on?"

"No, and I do not want any of this stuff turning up on the Internet or whatever, don't want that at all."

"I just don't know what to do."

"Just as a matter of interest, Barbara dumped him, what happen with you?"

"I went abroad for a year with my husband, that put an end to things." Elaine played with the DVD's. "So this is it, my shameful past, I should destroy them really, might watch them first, ooh I'm such a slut."

"Aren't we all."

"I'm not."

"Don't believe him Elaine, he's worse than both of us, the things he make me do."

"Like what?"

"Well you could always ask, I'm obviously up for it, if this shit is anything to go by."

"Oh Christ who has got this stuff?"

"Elaine, you are his neighbour, didn't you see anything? I mean you saw us."

"N reg Clio, round here."

"Oh thanks."

"You know what I mean."

"Yes I'm afraid I do."

They reset the alarm, Barbara and Elaine exchanged numbers and Andy put the two hard drives into the back of the neighbourhood lowering Clio. The pair then adjourned to Barbara's new home and proceeded to view countless gigabytes of home made porn, mostly on fast forward. Each woman had her own little folder, filed in chronological order and then named. Many of the starlets knew they were being filmed but it was obvious that in just as many cases some remained blissfully unaware. There were over fifty folders in all starting in 1979 with a scanned Polaroid of a blonde girl labelled "Sally" and progressing through the years and various technologies to Barbara and then an older lady called Gwyneth, (only three films of her) and on to a young woman, or rather a girl called Sharon.

"We should not be watching this."

"Totally immoral."

"Go back to Tracy, she was funny."

"I do believe she knew the camera was there."

"Oh hang on, look." Barbara pointed to the laptop. Two folders above Tracy was another Gwyneth.

"Open that." This particular Gwyneth had been

around for quite a while, at least a year, there were many, many films of her and she definitely knew the camera was there. They had been at it all over the place, indoors, outdoors, behind doors and in doorways. The folders were dated from 1983 until 1987. Roger had been a very busy boy in the eighties; he did rather seemed to have peaked there.

"A very new romantic."

"That's the same Gwyneth, twenty years before."

"Oh god, it is, well your are a dirty old whore."

"So much for the sister hood."

"Are there any addresses?"

"No but I bet he's got a record of you all somewhere. Probably on the DVD's."

"How many Zappa cd's are there?"

"Hundreds."

"Really!"

"Have a look on the internet."

"No I want to watch Tracy again."

"This is bad, we shouldn't, oh go girl, wow!"

"Morally wrong, wind it back, Jesus!"

"And again, oh dear."

After a while, a considerable while they got bored.

"We should delete all this stuff."

"After we have transferred it to this here hard drive of mine."

"Andy we shouldn't."

"Might be needed as evidence." Barbara plugged the cable in.

"We really should delete this." She dragged the contents over and dumped it into the appropriate file; funnily enough it did not say, "recycle".
"They are not having me for evidence."
"Not Anne."
"Not Jane."
"Some buggers got the DVDs of them anyway."
"Oh thanks for reminding me."

Deep in the heart of Disneyland Paris Roger's mobile was going bonkers, so utterly bonkers he turned it off. Several women of his acquaintance wanted explanations and they wanted them right fucking now. He managed to feign a dickey tummy and sat out the rides frantically texting and making excuses. The only words rattling around his head were. "Oh shit!"
Contact with Barbara had been established, unlike the other women she didn't want to kill him, see him burn in hell for all eternity; yes, but not kill him (not yet). Through a series of texts and calls they managed to establish that nine different ladies were not feeling all that positively disposed towards their former paramour. Barbara pointed out that he was lucky it was so few; after all, she had been through the hard drive. Between them they managed to work out which Zappa Cd's were missing. All they had to do now was become detectives and ascertain who had been in his library. Obviously all the women who had made

their little moments of movie magic there, but of them it would only have been the last two, unless someone was holding a huge grudge. Roger confessed to there having been a bit of a crossover between them. There was also, his wife, her friends, his children, their friends, the cleaning lady, and the cable guy.

"Pretty much any bugger who has been in the house in the past few weeks."

"That would be it."

"God Roger, you are such a twat!"

"I'm beginning to realise that now."

They tried to establish some sequence of events. The last little filming had been two weeks ago with the young lady labelled "Sharon". The first thing to do was find out if Sharon had received any letters. When it turned out that the only Sharon residing at her presumed address was in fact a three-year-old, Roger's feigned illness took a turn towards reality. He was loosing it and for a man so completely in control of every aspect of his life, this was not a good thing. Over the next day he became so morose and pitiful his that wife filled him full of painkillers and shoved him on a cheap and cheerful flight back home. She wasn't having him moping about being sick all the time and having moody tantrums ruin her and the children's holiday. Home James and don't spare the horses.

Barbara and Andy collected a very gaunt and pale Roger from the airport.

"My you look gaunt and pale."

"For a man who has been in the sun."

"Gaunt and pale this is Andy by the way."

"Andy, Roger, Roger, Andy."

"Not the legendary "Big Rodge", porn star and corruptor of this nations youth."

"The very same, if you throw up in this car we are dumping you by the road side, got it."

Roger was a shade of light green, possibly somewhere between "Bathroom jungle mist" and "Astro white with a hint of mint" if one was to look on the chart. By the time the little Clio lowered the tone once more he had swallowed several soup spoons of bile and a few lumpy bits, he was also aware of just how Andy felt about him and his antics and his sole excuse of; "You would have done the same if you had the chance." Was met with a tirade of abuse and a series of possible ramifications, none of which seemed all that pleasurable.

"Anyway, never mind how I feel about it; you have a bunch of irate women wanting to kill you, or at the very least, see you dead or as near as. I've never been one for friends reunited, there is usually a good reason you loose touch, but this I'd pay to see. We could start a new web page. "Deputy Heads Knock Offs dot com"

Barbara joined in.

"We have got the hard drives, we're going to make you a star boy! Not with me obviously, that's in the either, except for those fucking Zappa Cds. We could just put up all the ones who didn't know there was a camera there, call it; "Here's me being fucked by a dirty perv dot com." How could you do this, some of these women have families and stuff, have you any idea what you have done?"

Roger gave up and turned sheepish, reality was kicking his teeth in, and it hurt. Once in the house he made for the study, only stopping to throw up a few times. Barbara made a cup of tea and she and Andy brought Roger's home entertainment system into life.

"That's a big telly."

"That's a very big telly."

"But somehow I don't get a thrill seeing "Coronation Street" in near as damn it life size, might as well have the actors in the room."

"I don't want to smell Vera Duckworth."

"Is she still in it?"

"No idea."

"Where are the hard drives?" Roger came back in; only looking ashen faced and ugly, twas a big improvement.

"Over there in the bag." Andy pointed at the table.

"You will find me missing, and a few others."

"You stole these, removed them without permission, I could have you arrested."

"Go on then, here use my phone; tell you what I'll do it myself, what's that number again? Nine, nine…"

"Ok, ok, point made sorry." He sat down.

"I think you should go to the police, it would mean almost certain incarceration for your good self, but it would put a stop to all this."

"Why would I go to jail?"

"How many of these women knew they were being filmed? Deputy head, pornographer, there's a tabloid tale. I'm sure you will find you have broken one or two laws there."

"Oh bollox." Roger put his head in his hands.

"I do hate to be practical and all that, but, are there any films on the stolen DVDs that were not on the hard drives?"

"Oh fuck off, I need to sort this out."

"And we are just trying to help."

"I don't need your fucking help."

"Going to kill your self then?"

"I'll give you a hand with that."

"I need to think."

"With your willy."

"I think it must be the last girl, you know the one that looks under age, the one with no address. How did you manage that? She's not some kid from school is she? I hope not, some stupid student, what the hell are you playing at?"

"Like you wouldn't"

"No I bloody wouldn't, shagging kids is never a good idea, you're a fucking teacher for gods sake, never mind the abuse of power, you are old enough to be her dad. Never mind all the irate husbands finding out about their loved ones sordid pasts; what about this girls father, he could murder you and get community service."

"Piss off Andy, this has nothing to do with you."

"Or maybe an asbo."

Andy stood up, "Fair enough, consider me pissed off."

"Wait for me." Barbara bent down close to the sickly mans ear. "If any of this gets out in anyway, if anyone even looks at me in a funny way, I will kill you, you know, dead! Understand? Right, time to go." She stuck her head back round the door, "And if you want any help from me you are going to have to ask very nicely; Bye." They left him to stew and before they had a chance to shut the door that nice lady from next door barged her way in. The first thing they heard was a huge crash, a similar sound to that of a huge flat screen telly being ripped from the wall and being hurled to the floor. Then the screaming started. It faded as they walked to the car and by the time they were inside and the engine was running they could barely hear a thing.

"What do you want to do now?"

"We could go home and you know, do stuff."

"Or we could have a shag."

"You girls are so romantic."

Barbara's phone rang for the ninth time and again she ignored it. Roger was leaving increasingly more desperate and frantic messages. After the twelfth she called back.
"Morning dick head."
"Sorry."
"Oh you'll need to do better than that."
"Very sorry."
"Not good enough."
"I need your help."
"Oh, what a shame."
"Please."
"You are such an arse, the all powerful Roger reduced to this, right then arse face, what do you wish to do?"
Roger had spent the previous evening calling all his ex co stars and either reassuring them that all was going to be well (which it probably wasn't) or enquiring into any untoward recent events; untoward events being specifically the arrival through her majesties postal service of pictures of dubious artistic merit. Luckily for Roger most of his ex paramours seemed to feel that the only untoward event to befall them of recent times was his good self re-acquainting with them. His sudden interest in their well being was well weird and the sound of his voice was the only black cloud on an otherwise spotless and perfect blue sky. Roger had

managed to narrow the field down to eight possible runners. Names and addresses, change of addresses, phone numbers, star signs and where's and when had all been carefully logged in Roger's magic filing system, the man had been meticulous, right here and right now he was beginning to wonder why.

The fist thing Barbara noticed when she met him for the hastily arranged lunch, was the black eye. Black eyes are rarely a thing of beauty but on a fifty something year old, otherwise elegant man, they are more than slightly incongruous. The bar was bright and airy and the noon sun blasted through the fake stained glass window and perfectly illuminated all the hues down the left hand side of Roger's face.

"Elaine."

"Cant say I blame her, she's got a lot to loose."

"So have I."

"But it's all your fault. You are a dirty fucking pervert and you lost the DVD's, what a git. The only reason I don't kill you right now myself is that I want those things back and destroyed, once that event has taken place I may reconsider my murderous intent, but I doubt it."

"Ok you want to kill me."

"Do not make light of this feeling, I am not joking, that black eye is nothing to the pain you are going to be on the receiving end of, death will be a small mercy, and very prolonged."

"But you are going to help me?"

"Anything that brings the day of your death a second closer."

"Barbara."

"No, as soon as I get my DVDs you are going to die, got it?"

"Barbara."

"Not kidding."

"Fair enough, but you said you may reconsider."

"Perhaps."

"But you will help me first?"

"Like I said."

"Anything that brings the moment of my demise closer, yes I got it. Ok. Right. I can't find Sharon. She's gone, disappeared."

"How did you find her, she's not one of your usuals."

"She was; is, probably was, a cleaner at the school."

"Trace her through the agency, I'll have the pork." Barbara put the menu down.

"Suppose I'll have to."

"She does look very young, and I'll have the pork."

"I've got the feeling her details may not have been genuine."

"I'll have the fucking pork, Roger; it's a cleaning job, probably cash in hand, fake name, no tax. I mean just how kosher is the agency. Lets face it you are the lowest possible bidder, you never ask too many questions as long as the job gets done and will you go and order the food, I'm starving."

They had another argument over the wisdom of hiding in plain sight; the Zappa Cds. Another heated discussion over who could have possibly known what were in the Cd boxes. The absolutely no one answer was utterly refuted by Barbara. She was of the opinion that it had to be someone and the suggestion that it could have been his wife was rendered moot by the fact that he was still breathing.

"I take it you are going to check all the missisis mail."

"Oh god, never thought of that, shit."

"Oh dear Roger I do believe that you are about to cry."

"I am not going to roll over and die for this bitch, I will find her."

"Then what?"

"Have her arrested."

"Then you wife will find out. Anyway, how do you know it's a woman, could be a disgruntled boyfriend or husband."

"It's a fucking woman, only a woman could be so cruel."

"Thanks."

"Ok, sorry, got any suggestions then?"

"Has he she or it actually done any thing illegal? Shut up, all that's happened is some pictures have been sent. It's not as if someone has been surreptitiously filming nefarious goings on. That probably is illegal in this day and age."

"You still haven't proffered a suggestion."

"Purely pragmatic and utterly criminal; find this Sharon bitch, beat the fuck out of her, get the DVDs then kill her."

"I'm not going to kill her, I'm not going to kill anyone."

"Why not?"

"I could just buy the DVDs from her, assuming it is her; it's just blackmail."

"Oh yeah, digital media, that's not hard to copy, could be millions of them by now."

"Bugger."

"As you say it might not be her, could be the other woman, the one from before. Gwyneth or whatever."

"It's not her, I've known her for thirty years, it's not her. She would not do this."

"Right, course not, some bugger is doing it."

"Not her."

"Don't rule it out. Your young cleaner, she works at the school, so she must have had a police check."

"No, not strictly in contact with children, casual labour."

"Cheap and not exactly legal."

Roger shrugged. "Cut backs in cleaning, we can buy more books, simple as that."

More shrugs.

"Anyway Gwyneth got a letter as well."

"Proves nothing, she could have sent it to herself. Only got her word for it."

"Barbara, it's the cleaning girl, Sharon or what ever her name is, she's the only one. She did extra work for my wife."

"Oh for fucks sake, you were shagging the maid, this you could have mentioned, could have bypassed a load of, well, bollox; Jesus man you are an utter arse."

The shrugging recommenced.

"Fucking twatty arsed sign language, does Gwyneth know about her young rival for your inconsiderable charms and are you still enjoying hers?"

"Yes and no."

"No and yes."

"So she will be pleased."

"She's not."

"Have you seen her since you got back?"

"Not yet."

"Oh that will be fun."

"Wouldn't come with me would you?"

"Fuck off!"

"Come on, you are involved in this as well."

"Suppose it could be a laugh."

"Only for you."

"Does she know about Shazza?"

"Don't know, she described some of the pictures, sounded like you and Anne."

"Was Shaz in the Zappa bunch? Coz she's not been sent to anyone, yet. I only know about her because we had a good trawl through your hard drives, god you are a dirty bastard some of those women were rough as a badger."

"I told you it's Sharon."

"Despite the fact that it serves you right we do need to find this bitch, I take it she will be of the opinion that you are still on your holls? You need to get to the agency; someone there will know her. Tell them there has been a payment cock up and she's due some residuals or something, money usually brings out the best in everyone."

"You always were a clever thing."

"I'm still going to hurt you, badly."

"Better than death."

"I haven't decided to reconsider yet. Where is this agency then? I always wanted to be in Charlie's Angels. I wish to pursue my line of enquiries."

"All the information is in my office."

"Well let's get gone then, go pay for this."

Roger fell into step, he realised that Barbara was probably right. If he went in search, Sharon would probably do a runner where as Barbara could make discrete overtures with out setting off the alarm bells and causing prematurely terminal results. The school was open wide and a surprising number of teachers were wandering around in a state of suspended bliss. (No kids). Information was retrieved and printed out and then Barbara realised she couldn't do it.

"Don't fucking wimp out on me now."

"No you twat, if she's seen the pictures chances are she could recognise me."

"You don't look anything like you used to."

"Not doing it."

"Well how the hell…"

"Andy; he can do it, got nothing to do with anything, if you know what I mean, you'll have to be fucking nice to him though, you were an utter twat the other night."

"Couldn't you ask him?"

"Bugger off. When are you seeing Gwendolyn?"

"Gwyneth, tonight."

"Gonna shag her?"

"Probably not."

"You are a deeply disturbed individual."

After much pleading and begging and grovelling Barbara agreed to be there when the face off took place.

She was late and the eye looked fresher than ever.

"Hello, you must be Gwyneth." A hand was proffered and a firm grip received.

"You must be the ginger school girl, I feel we know each other already."

"Oh that was a nasty look, and please can I have my hand back, come on we are all in this together, we need a way out of this shit. Did you know about the Zappa Cd boxes?"

"No, all I had were some videos and a memory or two, then I ran into wonder-prat here and now my life is shit."

"I know the feeling, just as my life was turning into what pretentious pillocks would call "a happy place" twat face here has to ruin everything, and why do I never get to hit him?"

Roger was glaring at Barbara in a "Please shut the fuck up way" and she decided to go along with it. Perching herself on the couch next to Gwyneth she picked up the envelope and emptied it onto the table. The first picture was of herself, it was immediately turned over, the rest were all familiar but far more explicit. There was nothing remotely erotic about these; this was just full on hard-core porn, not nice. Barbara put the pictures in a pile, taking the ones of her and ripping them in to very small pieces. Roger began questioning in a cack handed nineteen fifties bad TV detective manner.

"For fuck's sake Roger shouting is not going to help, she knows nothing, look everything is the same, same note, same message, and same old bollox."

"Roger you make me sick, Barbara could you give me a lift home? I'm not staying here. How many lives have you ruined?" She stood and put her coat on. "I'll get a bloody taxi then, staying here for a shag then?" Barbara was glared at. "Get the cameras out." She picked her bag up as Barbara stood.

"No, no, I'll give you a lift, come on." It was not Barbara's turn to give the withering glare of impending doom, but she was getting better at it. Gwyneth's rage started to manifest in the car where she tore into her former lover, all the way across town and for seven miles on the bypass and she didn't pause for breath until the coffee had been poured. After a little sip she was off again. The tirade of abuse was rather intricate in it's formation, she had obviously had great deal of time to think it through, probably been practicing as well. Barbara sat and added the odd "Yes I know" and "Mmm" but the "Are you sure he's that bad?" sent the mad bitch off into another realm of insanity. The coffee making devil woman fell into a spiral of such venom that she, if not careful, could end up biting her self. Barbara's comment that Gwyneth seemed quite happy in the photographs, indeed definitely a willing participant, did not go down well. Many, many tears later Barbara managed to extricate herself. On the way out Barbara noticed a photograph, a familiar face but a little younger.

"Oh, who's this then? She looks nice."

"That's my daughter, she's at uni now, very proud of Sharon, beautiful girl, wonderful daughter."

"You should concentrate on that, think about the good things and all will not seem so bad."

"You are probably right, thanks for listening, and sorry for going on and on, oh god what if my daughter sees these pictures?" The tears began welling up again. Barbara made her excuses and left. She had some outrageous gossip for Andy.

"Oh dear, oh dear, oh dear." She thought as she started her little car.

"You're not joking are you, you are sure about this?"

"Utterly, and there she was, the proud mother."

"And what about daddy?"

"The woman's been divorced for years, went back to her maiden name, not that keen on men in general at the moment."

"She's going to kill him when she finds out."

"I think she's going to kill him anyway, save me the bother."

Barbara explained her little plan for luring Sharon into the open.

"Couldn't you just get her mother to call?"

"If I'd been making porno movies, ok, since I have been making porno movies the last person I would want to find out about it would be my dear mother, the only thing worse would be to discover she had been enacting the very same nefarious deeds with the very same chap. I feel we should at least try and avoid any hideous embarrassment at this stage in the game."

"Good point, well made, so you just want me to go to the agency and ask for Sharon specifically. What for, it's not as if I need a cleaner, shut up. That would be a bit off, not to mention odd. I just go in bold as brass and say Roger's wife recommended her; that's not going to work."

"No, say you are from the school and that some cash has been found or she's won the raffle or something. No, that's good, say that all the cleaners were automatically entered, tell them it's a couple of hundred of quids worth of shopping vouchers and all she's go to do is sign for it. We just need to find her and then we can follow her."

"This is all getting a bit "Eddie Shoestring""

"Have you got a better idea?"

"Get her address from her mum."

"How?"

"Go and see her, you want to be a detective, there's bound to be a phone number somewhere, have a look around, steal her mobile, I don't know."

"I do, and we do it my way."

"Which seems to involve me in all sort of deception, thanks a bunch."

"I'll wait in the car."

"Super."

"Just go to the agency and get a bloody number for me."

"Call them up."

"Tried that, they don't give them out, it has to be official. Someone from the school needs to do it, I know you don't work there but they don't. I can't go, Roger can't go; she knows him. I can't because she might recognize me, I've seen pictures of her, she may have seen some of me. It has to be you or we are all bolloxed, Roger can make up the ID cards and give you an official school letter, it'll be ok. Come on you can do it."

"I could just let you keep doing that and then say no."

"But then you would feel guilty."

"Nope."

"Why not?"

"You are trying to entice me into your diabolical scheme by means of sexual shenanigans."

"So."

"Don't you feel guilty?"

"Ok, I'll stop."

"I didn't say that."

"So?"

"I'll do it, just keep, oh that's it, that is definitely it."

The morning after, two plans were hatched. Andy collected all the relevant bumf from Roger; he was now a history teacher called Raymond Charles, even had a laminate that said so. He also had a very official letter explaining the raffle and the winning there of. All he needed was a signature and an address and the vouchers would be forthcoming. Barbara paid another visit to Sharon's mother and during one of her increasingly more elaborate reasons to be left alone, found a phone book.

Andy told Roger about the mother daughter predicament, the news did not go down well. The word shit was uttered more than once.

With the relevant documentation Andy was able to procure an address for the elusive Sharon. The promise of a huge raffle prize sliced through the red tape. He tried to feel guilty but couldn't, subterfuge was evidently in his soul. Sharon would not be receiving her non existent raffle prize any time soon.

Armed with the address Andy and Barbara consulted their trusty A2Z and drove round to have a look. It was an end terrace with no off road parking, recently double- glazed and had a "for sale" sign on it's end wall. They phoned the building society for details. It had been partially refurbished, had new central heating and was very much reduced in price for a quick sale. The present tenant was not the owner but there would be no problems as she was just looking after the place until it left the market. If they were interested all they had to do was make an appointment and someone from the office would meet them and show them around. The appointment was made.

Mid morning the following day the agent met what he considered to be the wettest couple in his living memory. The pair could not shut up, engagement parties, wedding plans, and local school facilities; they wanted to start breeding ASAP. The continual all round love fest made him feel physicaly sick, where did these idiots come from? He was sure this was going to be a quick and easy sale. Barbara made a huge fuss in the kitchen with a little note-book and a tape measure, checking all the sizes against the printed bumf. The agent explained that the present occupier was basically house sitting and could be gone as soon as required. She had very little in the way of personal belongings; just some clothes, a small television and DVD player and one of those little Cd players that look like an aliens head. Other than the small pile of Cds and DVDs there was very little else. The house was sparsely furnished, two of the bedrooms were empty, the other had a futon bed, there was an old Ikea couch in the front room and a plastic garden table in the dining room. The kitchen had had a little more care and attention lavished upon it, new cooker, fridge freezer and washing machine. Barbara made this point over and over until the poor man got so sick of hearing it that he took Andy outside to get away from the woman. Andy had a long list of questions about local amenities and such like and was determined to ask each and every one of them. This gave Barbara fifteen minutes alone. Fifteen minutes where she was able to rake through the pile of cinematic and auditory splendour. Amongst the Boyzone and Take That there were a few most incongruous Frank Zappa Cds. These she stuffed in her handbag, leaving the boxes in place. She returned to the kitchen where Andy was now enjoying a cup of tea and began making a detailed plan of the master bedroom. Handing the measuring tape to Andy she made it clear that she was going to start asking the most banal and utterly pointless questions. The agent elected to go with Andy and assist with the measuring.

Barbara took a cup of hot water through to the front room, opened up the laptop, checked there was no disc, plugged it in and emptied the water onto the keyboard. Just to make sure she gave it a good shake. After pressing the power button and holding for ten seconds she returned the machine to it's rightful place by the telly. Job Jobbed Barbara joined the two men upstairs where she began wittering on about a piano. The agent was beginning to imagine strangulation or suicide; he wasn't sure which one would be easier. He was saved from his imminent decision by the piano. The argument had escalated to the point of shouting; the piano was indeed a huge bone of contention for this otherwise seemingly perfect couple. By the time they left the house the shouting had abated and we were onto the stony silence. The non-committal monosyllabic grunts convinced the agent that there would be no sale today.

"Have you even got a piano? Can you play the piano? What the fuck was that all about?"
"No piano, but I do have some Zappa cds."
"How many?"

"All of them."

"Did you get a look at the laptop?"

"Killed it."

"How?"

"Boiling water."

"Bit harsh."

"You are not the one on the discs."

"We had better give them a good look anyway, just to make sure."

"God you are such a pervert."

"Yet I'm not on the discs. Oops, I unreservedly apologise for that callous and ill judged comment."

Barbara said nothing.

"Oh dear, is this a real stony silence?"

"No I'm just wondering if she made copies."

"Did the laptop have a DVD writer on it?"

"Dunno."

"Well it looked a bit cheap and didn't have much of a memory and there was no sign of an external hard drive. Did you check what was in the other boxes?"

"Yip, exactly what it said on them."

"She could have transferred it all to an i pod or something."

"Oh thank you, just when I thought it was safe to go back in the water. How do you know if she's got an i pod?"

"Everyone's got an i pod."

"We will have to nick it."

"They say the first one is the hardest."

"What are you on about?"

"Murder."

"What!"

"This is how it starts; nick her i pod, then kill the bitch, I know your sort. Anyway we don't have to nick it."

"Just dunk it in some boiling water."

"Or reset to factory settings, could have done that to the lap top."

"Boiling water was way more fun, it sizzled and everything. I just want to make sure that all those images of me never see the light of day."

"Someone is going to have to make friends with her. Can't really be me and Roger is totally out of the question. You need to get hold of her, talk to her."

"Fuck that, let's just do it to her, we have pictures of her, let's send her a letter."

"She's probably got one."

"Well she can have another."

"Then you can do your acting bit, you know All the "We're all in the same boat, bla, bla, bla."

Barbara thought for a while.

"Ok but we keep it to ourselves."

"Send her a picture of her mum."

"That's just cruel."

"Just to see if she acknowledges it."

Chapter Four

In which life goes on and our heroes do very little,
but other people do loads, so don't worry.

That evening Barbara and Andy printed up a few
little snaps from their recently acquired and
extensively pornographic files, the ones that had
not been placed in the recycle bin. The package
they made up contained some utterly disgusting,
nothing left to the imagination, pictures of Sharon
herself, two of her mother, one from years ago, one
more recent and one slightly saucy picture of
Barbara. Andy spent ages cutting up newspapers
and attempting to recreate the original note, then
gave up and stuffed the real thing in the envelope.
They printed off a duplicate set, with a few more
pictures of Barbara and posted them off on the way
to the pub. All they had to do now was to engineer
a meeting with Sharon, preferably with Roger and
Sharon's mum present, then light the blue touch
paper and retire. Barbara wasn't too keen on this
idea, as the fall out from such an event would
inevitably stain her otherwise exemplary character.
They would just; or rather Barbara would just have
to bump into her. What would be convenient to
know was whether Gwyneth was aware of Roger's
dalliance with her daughter? Andy's suggestion
that they should just go round and show her the

pictures was rejected on the grounds that it would be cruel and unusual (and never mind how funny).

The next morning was spent ignoring Roger's frantic calls and grunting gently to each other as they fought over the covers. Between the grunts they decided an holiday was in order, a dirty weekend was too easy, that they could do at home, they needed sunshine and sea and stuff, sunshine and sea and stuff and very soon, next week ish, seemed like a good idea. It would give them four more days to find out what was going on, four more days until Roger's family came back and the shit hit the fan big time. Barbara had decided that if it wasn't cleared up by then she was going to die her hair and deny all knowledge of anything to do with this series of unfortunate events. (And beat this shit out of anyone silly enough to suggest that the woman in the pictures and films looked a little like her, as if she would ever take part in such nefarious activities.) And if it ended up on the Internet she would just kill Roger, simples! While Andy was sure that the recovery of the Zappa Cds and the drowning of the laptop would save her from internet fame. Barbara was still a bit paranoid about the possibility of there being numerous copies of her epic performances. She was sure that Sharon had transferred all to her i pod. Andy pointing put that she may not even posses such a thing was met with the same derision as last time (except the other way round).

"I bet she's got an i pod, everyone's got an i pod and I bet she's got Pyromania on it."

"What?"

"Pyromania, deaf kitty."

"Yes I know, that's going back some, bloody hell, is it relevant?"

"She probably set fire to my house, old house."

Later that same evening Barbara sat dumfounded as she watched Andy doing his very best Eric Clapton impression; ok she tried not to yawn too much. The house band were really rather good but the odds and sods that gathered to demonstrate their god given musical prowess at this particular jam session left a little to be desired. Like a mini X factor, some were good, some were great but most were just drivel. Tonight's prize went to the pair of clueless morons who couldn't find the key to anything, let alone the pitch. The fighting was just an added bonus. Each blamed the other and neither would yield. Andy explained to them that the small PA system at their disposal could not possibly deal with their individual vocal prowess. This seemed to calm them down until one of them overheard someone mumbling about actually singing into the microphone. Andy just left them to it.

"Bet you just live for these moments of musical synchronicity."

Barbara gestured to the inebriated inbreds at the bar, they were still arguing but the blows had stopped. The petit bar maid had informed them that one more punch would mean eviction and she looked as if she meant it.

"Entire minutes of endless fun." Andy unplugged his beaten up old Strat and placed it lovingly in it's case.

"You don't treat me that gently."

"Oh that's good, coming from little miss "I'm not made of china you know." Make your mind up girlie."

"Oh piss off, come on, it's chips and cheese time."

"That's what's so good about you, the healthy eating."

Barbara crossed the road to the world's best chips and cheese emporium, it sold other things, like pizza and kebabs but the chips and cheese were straight from heaven sent, it smelt good as well. Andy put the change in his pocket and took the hot polystyrene box in his hand. His other was busy with the tomato sauce. They sat in the car eating their most romantic meal so far, twas bliss.

"You do realise we have booked ourselves a romantic holiday in Malta, two weeks."

"Yip, yum, yum, we will probably fall out by then."

"Almost certainly."

"Just as well it was cheap as chips then."

"For that price and I can put up with you for two weeks."

"Must be mad."

"That's just you."

"Shut up."

"Yes dear."

The nice post lady delivered the brown envelopes containing the horrid pictures at eight thirty six and nine fourteen. Barbara knew what was in hers and just stuffed it in her bag. She and Andy drove round to Sharon's temporary abode and waited. The front room window was open and the sights and sounds of life were oozing through.

Inside a very worried Sharon was weighing up her choices. She knew that she had not sent the envelope to herself, but it was to all intents and purposes just the same as the ones she had posted to others. Other than her good self the only person with access to the compromising material was her old fuck buddy Roger. The same Roger she had been studiously ignoring and avoiding for the past few days. The arrival of this particular envelope meant that she would now have to get in touch with him. Sharon was not too keen on pictures of her self indulging in a spot of afternoon how's your father seeping through to the general and great unwashed. Her little scheme, it would seem, to elicit some readies from Roger, was not as watertight as she has assumed. Some other bugger had the pictures.

The screaming started at the exact moment the empty Zappa Cd case hit the wall. Three and a half minutes later a sound, not too far removed from that made by a laptop being hurled across the room by a seriously disgruntled crazy woman, could be heard all along the street.

"Ooh, Missis!" Andy said. They were parked across the road and three houses back, their plan was to follow Sharon and for Barbara to seek some opportunity to engineer a meeting and give it her Baffta winning best; "Oh my god it's you, I recognise you, from these…" and waggle the envelope in her face.. "This is so embarrassing but..", or something along those lines.

After ten minutes of headless chicken time Sharon composed herself and called Roger's mobile.

"Oh my god, where have you been, I've been trying to get hold of you for days."

"Thought you were in France."

"Well I came back early, look I need to see you ASAP, can we meet, like I said ASAP!"

The realisation that his world was about to, not only fall apart, but to utterly disintegrate was dawning far too rapidly on Roger. His orderly controlled little universe was spiralling out of control and there seemed very little he could do about it. Three more days and it would all be over, three more days and his wife was coming home. He needed to get a bit of a rush on if he were to survive.

Andy followed the little Fiat into town and after dropping Barbara off, as soon as it was out of view, parked in the same multi story. Barbara followed the bleached blonde bob into the huge shopping centre and was just gearing up to bump into her when she spotted Roger in McDonalds. She held back and watched as the movie stars met. No kiss on the cheek, no handshake, just glares and distrust from both sides.

Barbara spent an age looking in the windows of the adjoining shops and whilst spying; learned that stuff in the pound shop was there for a reason, Accessorise really was a load of crap and she just needed those shoes. Inside the world's most omnipresent fast food emporium there was much pointing and silent anger, many "how could you do this to me" looks and at least one "For god's sake will you be quiet." If Barbara could have heard, or had she been able to tear herself away from the shoes, she may have gleaned, through the art of backwards lip-reading, she was seeing a reflection after all, some of the following.

"My bloody mother, you have been shagging my bloody mother, what a thrill for you, what a conquest, you're a shit Roger. Where did this come from?" She waggled the envelope. "Who else has got this stuff, you swore to me that this would be safe, just us and no one else will ever know, you bastard!" But her reverse lip-reading skills were a bit crap, must have been lack of practice, so all she did was keep the pair in view, in the reflection provided by the shoe shop window. She had to try them on. Venturing within she was able to make out "Fuck off Roger"; her skills were improving. The little cardboard box of French fries was emptied over a not too gentlemanly gentleman's head just as Barbara was doing up the second ankle strap. She had a small moment of panic and decided that trying on high heels whilst on a surveillance mission was definitely a no-no. However neither Sarron nor Roger stood up or made any other move that would cause any self-respecting private eye to assume they were going to make tracks. The gods were with her and so were the shoes. She paid cash, threw the rope tie bag over her shoulder and exited shoe heaven with her very own little slice.

Blatantly walking past the window where her prey sat, she ignored Rogers petrified frozen smile and headed for the bookshop on the opposite corner. From the self help section she had a clear view and could invisibly survey the goings on within the orange junk food emporium. There was still a great deal of gesticulating but sadly no more food attacks.

Sharon sat and listened to all Rogers hastily invented excuses, contrived reasons and explanations. Some DVDs had been stolen from his home office. The fact that Roger was sure that the perpetrator was sitting opposite him he kept to himself. He was sure; certain beyond doubt, that none of the stolen DVDs contained any off his little

trysts with the bottle blonde bobbed one before
him. The fact that his little chip thrower was
unquestionably the thief he kept to himself. He
hadn't put any of her little starring roles onto DVD,
they had gone straight to the hard drive. Roger was
sure that his little junk food junkie was attempting
to perpetrate an elaborate double bluff. He
convinced Sharon that he had no idea that Gwyneth
was her mother, which to start with had been true,
to start with. He was secretly rather proud of the
double conquest and that he had once managed to
do both of them in the same day. This disgusting
thought conflicted with his panic urge. Tempting
though it was, beating the truth out of the little
bitch was out of the question. So sure was he of
Sharon's guilt that he had spent most of the
previous evening editing out and blurring any
recognizable feature that could be mistaken for
himself from the little epics, oh the wonders of
micro soft. His plan was to blackmail Sharon into
returning his DVDs by threatening to expose her.
He had even begun constructing the website. Now
that Sharon had received some embarrassing
pictures he was at a bit of a loss. It was all getting a
little too complicated. As for Sharon, she was sure
the pictures had not come from her copy of the
disc; she'd kept that safe. She'd checked and
double-checked that; it was still in her handbag.
Sharon was very good at playing the wounded not
so innocent, so good in fact that Roger was

beginning to wonder. He'd been a teacher for so long that he was sure he could spot a liar at twenty paces but since joining senior management he had become so embroiled in his own lies that his bullshitometer had taken a few knocks and was not as accurate as he would have liked. It was the uncertainty that annoyed him the most, that and why had no one asked for any money? Why wasn't the little cow clearing out his bank account? Roger could see that he was getting nowhere with his not so subtle line of enquiry, as could Sharon with hers. Roger flicked through the pictures again and one stood out, as the sore thumb it was. The only non - pornographic one had been of Barbara, still a pretty foxy picture, sexy enough to be a genuine part of the bunch, but not full on. Barbara and that twat Andy were the only others to have had access to the hard drives and she had just walked past, complete with inscrutable smile. Were they going to blackmail him? His spiral of depression quickened. His utter helplessness in the face of complete annihilation was beginning to drain any fight that he had left. All he knew now was he'd have to find Barbara. He was almost chasing his tail in hell but at least he had some kind of plan. Sharon had none. She thought she had managed to divert attention from herself but she still had no clue whom had broken into her house, taken her stuff and broken the laptop. Then it dawned on her, no one had broken in; someone had been shown around. First stop for her would be the estate agents. Roger, standing in the face of certain death (when his wife found out…) decided to skip around it and find Barbara.

Barbara was getting sick of the self-help bullshit and was relieved when the pair of star-crossed lovers left the emporium of greasy delights. There was no farewell kiss and the two went their separate ways.

Barbara set off in pursuit. She had some vague plan of banging into her with the sole intent of being recognised as the subject matter in one of Sharon's pictures. She hadn't thought the thing through when she passed her quarry and turned sharply, almost knocking her over.

"Oh my god, I'm so sorry, are you ok?" There was much apologising and had they been in cars, insurance documents would have been exchanged. Barbara was in full flight but Sharon would not take the bait, she launched into plan B.

"My god it's you, sorry but do you know a chap called Roger? Look I received some, well, interesting pictures in the post this morning. Somewhat compromising pictures, mostly of me but I could swear there were some of you in there as well. It does look like you, I'm sure it's you."

"It's not me, I have never met anyone called Roger, go away you mad bitch!"

"No, no, it's you, look I've got the pictures here."
Barbara produced the envelope and started to open
it.
 "Not here, you stupid cow, bloody hell, alright
come on."
 Sharon apologised for her outburst over a coffee,
one of those chain coffees, in a chain coffee house.
 "I always think these place should have more to do
with Star Wars."
 "I hate Star Wars."
 "That's two things we have in common, Roger too
hates Star Wars."
  "Oh my god you are the school girl."
  "Fame at last, any sign of little lover boy?"
 "As far as I know he's in France. When did you,
oh you said, this morning."
 "Do you think it's him sending them?"
 "Why would he do that, he's in most of them?"
 "Good point, but when I get hold of him I'm going
to rip his balls off."
 Barbara began to take some pictures from the
envelope.
 "Not in here!"
 "Oops good point, there's another woman in my
batch, an older woman, you know even older than
me. Any idea who she could be?" Barbara slipped
the picture of Gwyneth onto the table-top. Sharon
flipped it over immediately.
 "Not in here, someone might see," She handed the
picture back. "I've got to go, an appointment,

look." Sharon scribbled her mobile number on a
napkin and passed it across. "If you ever see the
bastard again, let him know his days are
numbered." This time she didn't even finish her
coffee. Barbara sat back and flipped her phone.
"It's her, defo, where are you?"
"Fopp, there's a bunch of Nick Cave CD's for two
bucks a pop."
"Thought we were going on holiday, shit sorry,
sounded like a girlfriend there, get what you like,
anyway besides the point and well off it. It's defo
the bitch, go on ask me how I know?"
"Ok, how do you know?"
"She said "Oh you are the school girl."
"So?"
"I didn't send her any school girl pictures." She
tapped him on the shoulder.
"As if by magic, where did you come from?"
"I'm an angel, so it must be heaven, bloody hell."
Barbara picked up a copy of "Mud's Greatest Hits"
by "Mud"
"Get this."
"Really?"
"God yes, bloke in a dress banging out cheesy pop
classics and Les Grey, what a star!"
"You liked Mud?"
"I was very young, and my dad was a bit mad, still
is, but god yes, still do and proud of it, all that glam
stuff, even Gary Glitter but you cant say that any
more." Barbara placed the Mud Cd on top of the

Nick Cave pile. "Are you getting these or what? Come on I'll buy lunch."

After the traditional and legally binding tradition of looking at the mornings purchases whilst delicately sipping upon the first drink and waiting for their edible consumables to arrive, Barbara phoned Roger.

"And you recon she's Gwyneth's daughter."

"Roger she is, there were pictures all over the flat, it's her kid."

It was not a pleasant call, Roger was beginning to shit himself big time. He had arranged to meet up with the blonde bob's mother that very afternoon and was a little worried that Gwyneth's reaction to his shagging her daughter might not be all sweetness and light. Other than the imminent return of his wife, this was top of his reasons not to be cheerful list. Andy and Barbara booked an appointment with his royal disgruntled ness.

"What do we need for this holiday then?"

"Hypnotherapy."

"Other than that?"

"Sun screen and mosquito repellent."

"You can get that stuff there, people actually do live there you know."

"Good point, just condoms then."

"People do live there you know."

"I know but it's hot, so what we need to do is get a big bag of willy socks, turn the heating up and practice."

Andy just looked at her.

"Get used to the climate."

He continued staring.

"Don't want to get too sweaty."

Andy just looked out of the window, Barbara kicked him under the table, rocked back and forth in her seat and said.

"Practice."

"Just in case we get it all wrong."

"Be a shame if we did."

"Better call a taxi then."

Chapter 5

In which our heroes save the bad guy and formulate a cunning plan.

As they turned into Roger's salubrious road Andy asked.

"Do you really not need to go shopping before we go away?"

"Oh course I do, but I'm not dragging your sorry arse round with me."

"Thank god for that. Right here we are." Andy turned the car into the drive and lowered the tone immediately. The door was open and they walked straight through to the sumptuous lounge, no signs of life awaited them.

"Roger." Nothing.

"He's got to be here somewhere, there's no way he would leave the door open, no way." A quick traipse round the ground floor proved fruitless, Barbara headed upstairs and Andy ventured into the garden. He heard her shout as he admired the plants in the green house.

"Andy get here quick." He ran into the house and followed the shouting. In the en- suite Barbara was calling the emergency services.

"I don't know the number, I'm a guest. I will give you the address once more, so that when he dies it will be your fault; your voice on the news, want to live with that?" She paused, gave the address again and explained the situation.

 Roger was passed out in the bath, the water was very red and his wrists were very cut. Andy raked through the cupboard and found some sticking plasters and several boxes of pills; empty boxes of pills. Painkillers, sleeping tabs, the usual, but it wasn't the parrot that had eaten them all. The pair of them struggled to drag Roger from the bath and wrap him in towels. Andy dried his forearms and began patching up the torn wrists as best he could. At least it seemed to stem the blood flow, a little. They took him down stairs and Barbara called nine, nine, nine, again and as she was explaining the urgency of the situation the ambulance arrived. The first thing the paramedics did was to rip off Andy's amateur attempt and dress the wounds in a more appropriate manner. Despite shining torches into his eyes and shaking his carcass, Roger did not seem to want to wake up. Andy told them about the pills and fetched the boxes and containers. Paramedic number one put them in a clear plastic bag then picked up the comatose deputy head as paramedic number two cleared the way to the ambulance. Andy was elected to remain and Barbara jumped in the back. This was new for her, not exactly like the movies but the siren was cool. Paramedic number one (whose name was Ralph and who collected stamps) looked through the clear plastic at the empty boxes and bottles.

"He seems pretty determined, even if we managed to stop the bleeding in time, once some of these get into the system." He shook the clear plastic bag. "It can all be a bit touch and go, mostly go to be honest. So what is your connection with out patient?"

"His name's Roger and I used to work for him, with him, whatever, just a friend now. Just a friend, seems so unimportant, suppose it is." Barbara answered whatever questions she felt like answering and notes were taken. No mention of the wife, not yet.

It took seven and a half minutes to reach the hospital and a further two and a half until the nurse pulled the screens round and asked Barbara to leave. She sat in the waiting room with the walking wounded, the stroppy drunks and the bleeding man hand cuffed between two of her majesties finest. A steady stream of self-inflicted drunken fools joined the queue. Barbara gave up her seat to a near zombie like teenage girl with what even Barbara could tell was a broken arm. Outside with the smoking wounded she called Andy.

"Still there then?"

"Is he going to be ok?"

"No idea, you should just lock up and go home."

"I was going to come and get you."

"My hero! I was hoping you were going to say that."

"I have found the keys and his wallet, shall I bring some clothes for him."

"Not sure if there is any point, but yes you may as well."

"What's going to happen, when is his wife back?"

"Couple of days."

"Wonder why he did it now then?"

"No idea, see you soon."

Andy stuffed some pants, socks, jeans, T shirt, and jumper into a Tesco bag, checked the locks, set the alarm and made his way, rather more slowly than Barbara, to the hospital.

Roger was stable, physically at least. Pumped and empty of all evacuable additives; he lay asleep.

"If he's got one of those clauses in his will, the do not resuscitate thing, he could do us for assault."

"What, for saving his life?"

"Yip, saw it on the telly, must be true."

"Do you think we should stay with him?"

"Don't think they will let us, anyway I think we have done our bit. I've written a note so that if and when he awakes from his suicidal slumber, he can make himself aware of what a stupid twat he has been. We will just, well I will just come back first thing and try and find out what the hell happened."

Suddenly aware of the ludicrous car parking charges levelled at the general populous in their hour of need Andy began emptying his pockets into the machine. He looked at Barbara.

"Don't start."

"Don't start what?"

"Wasn't going to but now you mention it, it is a bit much charging the good people of this fair nation astronomical amounts for the privilege of visiting their sickly relatives, bloody scandal."

"Good, I'm glad you think that way."

"As all right thinking folks should and probably do."

"Indeed, how are we going to get the little slut to confess her sins?"

"Which one? There's so many."

"Sluts or sins?"

"Both, oh it's her, the bitch Sharon, it's bloody her."

"Must be, she knew you as the school girl, unless it's on the Internet already."

"Oh don't say that."

"Don't you look worried?"

"And if it was you?"

"Good point."

"She looked really worried when I saw her, really worried. Not just someone's got hold of the DVDs and broken my laptop worried, but really worried."

"You mentioned that, really worried."

"Sort of; if this gets out my life is over worried."

"Not; oops I've forgotten to feed the cat worried."

"Slightly more worried than that."

"Like really worried."

"Yip, really worried."

"Has she got a cat?"

"Not just a big.."

"Shut up! You were actually going to say that, bloody hell."

Back at chez Andy, the cathode rays did their trick, but just before they nodded off Andy though out loud.

"Why would she send pictures of her mother?"

"Oh go to sleep."

"No, there were loads of others she could have used, why her mum?"

"I don't know and at the moment I don't care, go to sleep."

After a few minutes of not sleeping, Barbara snuggled into Andy's shoulder.

"She must be shitting herself, like me she probably thought the stuff was safe, she had it, he had it and that was that."

"The stuff?"

"Her adventures in Lolita land."

"She's not exactly Lolita."

"Oh you know what I mean, the shaggy fuck films, so when a third party, i.e. me, sent her some, what ever plan she may have had went fluttering out the open window."

"Plan gone ever so slightly askew, even."

Barbara raised herself up onto her left hand and looked down at her understanding bloke.

"I think she was going to blackmail him, she had all that stuff, the last thing Roger wants is a bunch

of irate women full of murderous intent after him.
He would pay a fortune to get those discs back."
"Are you suggesting we blackmail him?"
"No, how much? No, nope and no, it's bloody
awful being on the wrong end of this."
"How much?"
"No! Just bloody no, oh bugger I'm all awake
now, you will have to help me sleep." Andy felt his
head being pushed under the covers.

Second thing in the morning (she owed him one)
they made their way to the hospital and found
Roger in the waiting room. He had managed to pull
through and convince anyone who pretended to
care that last nights little escapade would not
happen again. He seemed genuinely pleased to see
them, and surprised, surprised to be alive. Those
who survive a life terminating procedure at their
own hands often do feel slightly relieved. Some,
quite a few go on to try again but some seem to
discover that the problem was not perhaps as
insurmountable as previously imagined.
"So are either of you going to ask me?"
"Nope; if I had spent most of my life filming my
excessive sexual exploits only to find that my
entire archive had been half hinched thus leading to
a career ending and possibly family shrinking
event, I too would probably top myself."
"Then you would be an idiot, it wasn't that."
"Will you just ask him?"

"You bloody ask him."

"I don't care."

"Ok, shut up, you don't care, good. I'm going to tell you anyway, listening; good, sitting comfortably; Good. Right; Yesterday I met up with Gwyneth and for the first time ever went to her flat. Now Gwyneth had never ever mentioned anything to me about her daughter, nada, nothing, knew nowt about her, and suddenly, there she is."

"Sharon was there!"

"No, pictures of her all over the place."

"And Sharon being one of your most recent knock offs, must have put you off your stroke."

"Don't be silly."

"Oh come on you knew what you were doing."

"Any way there's all these pictures of Sharon looking at me, eyes following me everywhere, like some horror film."

"I don't get it, you needn't acknowledge your recognition."

"Acknowledge your recognition, oh Andy you know such big words."

"Shut up, bloody hell I'm trying to explain, it gets worse. Gwyneth started crying and blubbing away, giving it the full soap opera dramatics, totally over the top; she used to be a drama teacher you know. I forgot that, she had me convinced."

"Convinced about what?"

"Oh yeah, em.. apparently Sharron is my daughter. Dun dun dun.."

"Andy, stop laughing, Jesus would you show some decorum. Roger there is no way that girl is your daughter; there is no resemblance what so ever. Oh "Eastenders", I just got the drum thing, very good, you seem a bit more cheerful about this now."

"Well she's not. No way, I realise that now, I realised that in the bath, but then I fell asleep. She's not even the right age, well she could pass for it, but she's not. If she were mine she would be at least twenty-three. Sharon is twenty-one, I've seen her passport, but my god that woman was convincing; she had me believing it. Had me thinking I had a daughter, not only that I had a daughter but that I had been shagging her."

"And filming it."

"Yeah, yeah, ok, anyway I convinced myself that it was all true and spiralled into the pit of despair. So thank you and thank you, but now I need to see the bitch."

"Which one?"

"Gwyneth."

"I'm pretty sure Sharon is in on it."

"No."

"She's been sending the stuff."

"Are you sure?"

"Oh yes, she knows way more than she's been letting on."

"Oh, I'd begun to think that it was all Gwyneth, oh bugger, what's going on?"

Barbara explained her theory, the machinations and consequent deductions and Roger agreed that all evidence seemed to point to the Sharon woman, but he was still quite sure that Gwyneth was involved in the plot somewhere along the line. It was now turning into what could only be described as a conspiracy theory. Why had the pair sent pictures of Gwyneth and not Sharron? Why the "leave him alone" message on Barbara's old house? And why had there been no demands for money?

"Why would anyone want you to be left alone, other than your not so good self?"

"Smacks of desperation that."

"Sure it's not your wife."

"It's not my bleeding wife, could you pair be slightly less insensitive? Come on I've just recovered from an attempted suicide, she would just kill me, and probably still will."

"It's hardly our fault that you are an utter nutter."

"Nope, we didn't fill ourselves with paracetamols and laxatives before slitting our wrists."

"Just as well you took the laxatives coz if that other muck had taken hold you'd be a bit dead, not just in dire need of nappies."

"Exit life."

"Enter darkness."

"Back to never-never land."

"Oh will you just shut up, bloody hell I've got a day and a half to sort this shit out before the family comes back."

"Last time I offered to help you…"

"I'm so sorry, I'm so fucking sorry."

"Are you sure, are you really sorry?"

"He does look a bit sorry."

"But is it enough?"

"For fucks sake!"

"Ok, Jesus wept, right we need a plan."

"A conspiracy type plan even."

"Whatever."

Andy's plan to set up a web site and reap the rewards did not go down too well, but at least it was a plan; probably a much better plan that the shambles they seemed determined to put into play.

Chapter six

In which our heroes put their cunning plan into action.

"So we are basing this on the assumption that Sharon recognised you as the kinky school girl, the pretty fucking sexy kinky school girl."
"Alright Andy, I get the point. I did not send her the school girl pictures so she must have seen them somewhere else, and... and she did have the DVDs, don't forget that; she did have the DVDs."

Back at Roger's house they made a time line of events. Not as hard as it sounds. Roger went on holiday and then the letters arrived, somewhere between these two events the mystery criminal mastermind appropriated the DVDs. It was agreed that this person was probably, definitely probably, Sharon. She had had both opportunity and access, the motive was probably blackmail; this was yet to happen. Roger was still convinced of the mother's compliance. She always had been a "mad bitch".
"You're the one who was shagging her."
"And filming it."
"Ok, can we accept that I am an utter arse and that no further recognition of this state of affairs needs to be endlessly brought up? Please!"
"Na, you are an arse."
"And we will repeat it."

"Over and over"

"Again and again."

"Arse."

"Ok. I'm an arse. You do know that I recently attempted suicide. You could push me over the edge again"

"So you are a twat as well."

"Thanks a lot Andy. Ok. Right; why would she claim it was her daughter, my daughter."

"Other than the fact that she's a nutter and she hates you."

"Good call Andy, I can understand that, I hate him; wish he was dead."

"I think it's all quite funny, with the exception of the seriously misguided suicide attempt, na, even that; Poo boy."

"I'm not too keen on ending up on the internet with old scrotum face here, that does not strike me as witty in the least." Barbara pointed at scrotum features, "Not at all amusing."

"I thought we had all the stuff back."

"Unless she made copies, everything seems to be in place, if that's all you guys have."

"I trashed her laptop, the old boiling water trick."

"Gwyneth is computer illiterate."

"You sure?"

"She can barely work her mobile phone."

"Looks like you are safe then."

"I think we are forgetting one tiny little thing here."

"What?"

"Someone tried to kill me! Set fire to my house, remember."

"Oh yeah, have any of your other co stars had a similar experience, direct action even? You have so much shit to sort out over the next..." Andy looked at his watch. "Before the missis gets back."

"And just how are you going to explain the scars?" Barbara pointed to his bandaged arms.

"Least of my worries, we'll have to, I'll have to sort it out, before Sunday lunch time."

"You need to confront Gwyneth, why would she tell you, or lead you believe that you are the little sluts father?"

"I don't want to confront anyone; I want it all to go away."

"Well it isn't going to, call her now, no time like the present, come on, man up."

Roger just sat and stared, and sat and went all a bit vacant really. Barbara clicked her fingers in his face, he barely registered; she did it again.

"Oh fuck..ok,, yes, your right, she's not going to go away."

"I'd like to know who burned my old house down, has this woman got a history of bonkers-ness?"

Roger's sharp intake of breath, rolling of the eyes and deep sigh seemed to affirm Barbara's supposition.

"Right, mad as a fish then." Andy continued. "Do we wish the police to become involved?"

"They already are as far as the house goes."

"But that does not involve our twat of a suicidal nutter here, on the surface that's just someone trying to get to you. Someone with a vendetta, oh that's a nice word; vendetta."

"We need her to confess."

"Oh very good Roger; duh! And just how are we going to do that?"

"Get her talking; give her a few drinks and she wont shut up, she cant shut up, god it goes on and on. I suppose I'll have to be nice to her, oh god not again."

"Again?"

"Years ago I had to pretend to offer her the earth and then go on to convince her it wasn't what she wanted after all, took months. Oh well, we will need to record it somehow."

"You seem to think this will be so easy, like she will fess up."

"She will, we just need to record it, evidence."

"Video?"

"Why not?"

"Seems awfully elaborate."

"Needs must."

"Why not just call her, a big long phone call, record it."

"She won't feel secure enough on the phone, I'll call her and be Mr. Wonderful, she'll soon invite herself over."

"You do seem very sure of your self."

"It's not me, she's just so bloody predictable, well perhaps not the trying to burn your house down and kill you stuff, but people don't change." Roger seemed in full control of all his faculties once more.

"She will rant and she will rave and she will scream and shout and threaten and scratch and bite but finally she will calm down and want to meet up somewhere."

"Metaphorical scratching and biting then."

"Yes, metaphorical, oh bloody hell, might as well do it here."

"Why not the pub?"

"We need to record the confession, we get that and we can make her go away."

"You think?"

"I hope."

"Get her here alone and there will be a great deal of tricky negotiating and unpleasant subterfuge, and that will just be me."

"You going to shag her?"

"No!"

"Why here?"

"She likes it here, she fucking loves it here."

"Probably thinks it should all be hers."

"And if he hadn't tricked her into dumping him all those years ago it could well have been."

"Ok team, practicalities."

"If he calls us team again, can I smash him in the face?"

"Right after I have kicked him in the balls."

Cameras were hidden away in places of unobvious predicament and all Roger would have to do was press the red button on and the evening's proceedings would be committed to the hard drive. Barbara and Andy stayed for the call. He was good. Hiding the seething rage behind a mask of even-tempered acquiescence, Roger explained this and that and begged to see her. He was worried that their little tape had perhaps gone astray, there had been a break in and some of his most treasured possessions had simply gone. The screaming and shouting and metaphorical scratching and biting hadn't lasted all that long. He soon had her reminiscing about the good old days and within twenty minutes she was on her way. Barbara and Andy wanted to stay but he was having nothing of it and kicked them out.

"He's going to shag her."

"I'm not going to shag her."

Chapter seven

In which all sorts of shit happens and it looks like our heroes might have a shag (in a very romantic way, so don't worry there's nothing crude going on here, no way, no how).

" The best of ELO! Is that it? Is that all we have got?"

"Bet you know every word of every song. Show me a man who claims not to like "Mr. Blue Sky""

"And I'll show you a liar. Yeah, yeah, I know. So that's it with old rockin' Rog then."

"Suppose so, he'll film their meeting and blackmail her into buggering off."

"Ooh what a plan, the man's a genius, what are we going to do now then?"

"Well I see the evening panning out something like this; we stop off at Tesco's, get a ready meal or something, bottle of wine, box of condoms head home and I use you as a sex toy until I get bored, then you can cook."

"Seems fair."

"What about romance? Tenderness? All that bollox! Good god you can go of folk you know."

"Twas your idea to use me as a sex object, the fact that I am prepared to hide my true feelings and go along with your sordid idea just shows how much I respect you."

"Utter shite, anyway it was sex toy, not sex object you tit. Your batteries are probably running low. Think I'll just kick you out here and get a meal for one in the lonely hearts isle, then go home alone and talk to my cat."

"You haven't got a cat."

"I'll rent one, you can get them in the isle next to the lonely hearts one, going to get a big ginger one, and if you make any feeble comments about big ginger pussies I'll wait till it starts raining and then kick you out."

"Tesco's is that way, where are we going? You've gone right round the roundabout, what's going on?"

"That was her, two cars ahead, good she's stopped at the lights."

"Who?"

"Roger's non existent daughter."

"Oh, don't let her see you."

The lights changed and Barbara did her best to stay at least two cars behind but never having had any police training soon found herself mere feet behind her quarry. Several "shit, shit, shits." ensued until Barbara managed to let someone pull out before her.

"Dinosaurs."

"What?"

"Do ya think she saw us?"

"Oh that's crap."

"Well my batteries are running low."

"I think she could well be heading for chez Roger."

"It does look that way, with this being his little street and her stopping right there." Barbara drove past, turned into the first available side road and pulled up. She gave Andy the "well what are we going to do now?" look as she opened the door. Andy returned with his "this is a really stupid idea!" glare, before opening his. By the time they had a clear view, Sharon had already crossed the road and was walking up the drive. Barbara crossed over and led Andy up a partially concealed alleyway. He stopped.

"Just what the fuck are we doing?"

"I want to see this, come on, that's what "the fuck" we are doing."

"This is not a good idea." Andy could have said this out loud but kept it to himself, he felt it would be better that way, anyway he too had an urge to have a right good nosey. Barbara seemed to know where she was going, so he followed on. Soon they were in the back garden and crouched behind the low wall separating the rockery from the conservatory. Through the plants they could see into Roger's front room and what a view they had, shame the sound had been turned down. An already weeping Gwyneth was doing her bit on the couch as Roger led in the spurious daughter. Sharon immediately started waggling her finger and mouthing off.

 "I'm all for the medium of mime but I have got to hear this." Barbara slithered across the path, in a rather noisy fashion it must be said but what stopped her from being able to hear also stopped those inside. The conservatory door just happened to be open. Barbara looked back and feigned surprise. Andy shook his head and mouthed "No" He then sat down with his back to the little wall, said "Oh fuck" to him self a few times before recommencing his spying activities. Barbara was now standing in the conservatory making stupid faces and doing an even stupider little dance. The "oh for fucks sake" expression on Andy's face was well hidden behind the bushes but Barbara knew it was there and she didn't care. She had now positioned her self in such a manner that she could partially see and fully hear what was going on.

 "Of course I'm not your fucking daughter, I'm not even her daughter, it was all a set up, just a plan to get some money. And it was all her plan, stop bloody crying for Christ's sake."

 Roger managed to persuade Sharon to take a seat and tried to civilise the situation by offering cups of tea. Two sugars and just a little milk and a "fuck off", followed by a request for a cup of coffee with a little milk, later and Roger was in the kitchen filling the kettle. Barbara stepped into view with

her finger over her lips and shrugged. She walked
to the door, being careful to keep out of sight.

"You said there would be a lot of money in this,
where is it? You fucking said, stop bloody crying
you silly old bitch. Fuck's sake, I better get some
money out of this, after what I've done. Just
fucking sort it out. And stop that over acting crying
shit."

Barbara mimed "oow" at Roger who mouthed,
"What are you doing here?" Barbara's little mime
got the point across, she had no idea and anyway
these games of charades would have to wait.
Barbara passed the milk over. Roger made a little
strangulatory gesture before picking up his tiny tray
and returning to the battlefield.

From her vantage point in the kitchen Barbara
soon got bored listening to the bickering between
the three ex's and started building herself a
sandwich. Gwyneth was still wittering on about
how Roger had ruined her life and Sharon just
wanted to know where the money was. Barbara had
to admit to herself, whilst adding the last of the
peanut butter to her almost Scooby Doo like edible
sculpture (it had been a long hard day and she was
a bit peckish) that she would never, had bothered
getting so emotionally het up over such an utter
arse. A bit of fun was a bit of fun but to waste your

life pining over a man called Roger, bloody Nora!

The man in her life had stopped following the events scrolling forth through the French windows and had become far more interested in the humongous bread based culinary monument his hearts desire was constructing, so much so that he didn't see the vase being thrown. He did hear the smash though. His attention once more riveted to the on going true life drama he wished his lip reading skills were up to the mark. The sound had been muted and the remote needed new batteries. (Obviously it wasn't really as bad as that, but you know, close.) Barbara could hear what was going on and if she had to summarise it would be something like this: Gwyneth was not happy at the way her life had panned out and she blamed Roger. Sharon was not happy at the way she had been used and wanted some money. Roger was happy that he had had so much sex with so many women, and that he had managed to keep a visual and auditory record of it all, bit of a shame the shit seemed to be hitting the fan at this particular moment but; hey shit's like that, it happens. Roger didn't actually say this out loud but he did think it and had been thinking of it nearly every day for the past twenty years, apart from the bit about the shit hitting the fan, that bit had never been part of the plan. What he did say was something about Gwyneth's husband. That was the point where the vase flew, weeeee..tinkle tinkle. That marriage hadn't lasted and guess who's fault that was? Roger didn't think it was but evidently he was wrong. Then there was the husband after that and the one after that and very nearly the one after that, but as that had never happened Roger could only be blamed for it not happening in the first place. Gwyneth's tirade had been well rehearsed and would have been utterly convincing if you were; a, drunk or; b, on the Gerry Springer show, or both. At this point none of the three protagonists were on the Springer show, only Gwyneth had misplaced the point to such an extent that she believed anyone could possibly be interested in her sad little life. She probably did have Jeremy Kyle's number in her bag. Sharon was rendered speechless by this misplaced logic for a good few seconds before resuming her quest for monetary recompense. (And the summarising part finished ages ago, in case you were wondering why it was going on for so long, it being a summary and all that.) Barbara had become bored again and had started in on her culinary delight, much to the annoyance of Andy who was out in the cold, and rapidly becoming colder, garden watching her stuff her face. Never the most elegant of eaters, unless in polite society, Barbara had managed to drop half the thing on the floor, there had been a soft splodgy sound as it hit and the noise a pickled onion makes as it rolls across lino, but neither of these were enough to interrupt the flow of utter crap pouring from Gwyneth's heart.

Roger made sure they all had what they wanted, in the tea department, not the money or the lurve department, they were on another floor entirely. He then proceeded to explain to Sharon that she could take the fridge if she really wanted. This was beyond all logical reasoning to the poor girl, what did a fridge have to do with anything? She didn't want a fridge, she didn't need a fridge, she wanted some money, quite a lot of money, and she wasn't going to spend it on a stupid fridge.

"What I am, in my round about way, trying to tell you is that I have no money, on the surface it would appear that we, or I, am rather well off, however despite the illusion of opulence conjured by my lovely wife's delusions of grandeur, it is all in fact just that; an illusion."

"What?"

"I'm skint."

"What?"

"Worse than skint, I'll show you my credit card bills if you want. If you have more than the price of a second hand fridge to your name then you are considerably richer than me."

"What?"

"The fridge is the only thing in this house that's actually been paid for. We are mortgaged to the hilt; even the groceries are on the credit card. That cup of tea you are drinking, or your coffee, hasn't been paid for yet. So if you want the fridge, take it, it's the only thing that's mine. Oh hang on it could be my wife's. Take it anyway, I have a sneaking suspicion that this particular life of mine could well be coming to an end, don't think I'll be needing that big a fridge in my bed sit."

"Oh my little heart bleeds for you, you bastard."

"Gwyneth, I'm not the one trying to blackmail someone here."

"I'm not trying to blackmail you."

"I am, fuck's sake, I want some money, you fucking told me there would be a great deal of money in this, you old witch."

"Hang on, if you're not trying to blackmail me, then what the hell are you doing?"

"I just want to ruin your life, the way you have ruined mine."

"How did I do that?"

"I….."

"We are not going through that again, shut up Gwyneth, just shut up."

"I loved you!"

Roger was suddenly reminded of the old Tina Turner song that had served as the soundtrack to one of their earlier videos, it had been on the radio at the time. But he also remembered that everything was being filmed and he for one did not wish appear to be anymore despicable than was strictly necessary.

"Well I can't do anything about that, I myself have a soft spot for Felicity Kendal but I fear that shall be for ever unrequited." The second vase narrowly missed Roger's head.

"Another thing that's still not paid for, doubt if I'll even be able to claim on the insurance."

"Oh shut up, you must have some money, if you don't cough up I'm going to your wife."

"Oh Sharon, I think we can safely assume that your "mother" here is going to do that anyway, so it kind of make's your threat redundant. I'm buggered, I'll probably lose everything, you know, the usual stuff; house, car, wife, kids, I'd say DVD collection but someone already has that." Roger tried to look wistful as he continued. "All my Frank Zappa Cd's."

In the kitchen Barbara was desperately trying not to laugh, Roger could be a witty old rogue.

"So sorry Shazza, no money from me, try her. Have you still got the DVDs by the way and if so, can I have them back? I'd like something to do in my forthcoming evenings of enforced solitude. All alone in my little bed-sit, with my one bar electric fire and my second hand toasting fork, I shall need something to remind me of days gone by. Then again as I'm going to lose everything I may as well stick them on the Internet myself, at least I'll be famous for something."

"Someone stole them."

"Oh great, that's all we need." Gwyneth glared at her former co-star.

"And I suppose this is my fault as well."

"If you hadn't made those bloody tapes."

"None of this would ever have happened, what a shame. Just let me get this straight. Sharon; you are attempting to blackmail me with what seems to be very little evidence what so ever. Well, no evidence what so ever. Would I be correct in assuming that? It appears I would. Well things don't look so bad after all. Perhaps all is not lost. You could try telling my wife but I warn you, I don't think she would believe you. You are very young and so very pretty and I'm, mmm, not. So I think she would consider you mad. Look at me, what on earth would a gorgeous creature like you want with an old scroat like me? Not really on is it. And Gwyneth I'm afraid that you are just a deranged old nut bag whom I happened to have known before I even met my wife. Tell her what you like, I'll deny it and just a little reminder to myself." Roger looked at the bookcase. "Edit this last bit out."

"What are you doing."

"Oh Gwyneth, have a fucking guess, he's filmed this. Bloody hell."

"Oh come on ladies, after all we have been through. Can't we just chalk it up to experience and get on with our lives?"

"Oh dear, it would appear not."

Andy saw it before anyone else. Sharon had reached into her bag and brought out a gun, one of those automatic pistols you see in American cop shows, not exactly Clint but; a gun is a gun.

"Where is the camera Roger?"

"Sharon! Where did you get that?"

"As if that matters, Jesus Gwyn."

"Get me the camera Roger, you old scroat, that's about the only thing you have been right about all evening. I want some money."

"I haven't got any." Roger handed her his all bells and whistles toy, after surreptitiously removing the link to the hard drive recorder. She took out the memory card and handed it back.

"See I can be reasonable, bet you haven't paid for that yet either. Right I want your car."

"Bet he hasn't paid for that either."

"Gwyn, she's got a gun, I'm sure she knows someone who can get rid of a stolen BMW for her."

"Oh, well done Sharon, well done."

"Shut up you old bag and get your credit cards ready, we are all going to visit a cash point. Roger darling, I'll be needing the documents for the car."

In the garden, behind his little wall, peering through the bushes, Andy, much to his surprise had taken out his camera phone, propped it against the bird table, checked the picture and decided to go and do something heroic. As he was crawling towards the kitchen he had a funny feeling that calling the police and running away would have been a better plan, it would in fact have been a plan and a good one. As the conservatory door drew closer he began wondering what on earth he was going to do. The foolishness of his self-imposed predicament reared its ugly head even higher when Barbara tripped over him and landed with an almighty crash into a pile of empty pots and a plastic watering can.

"Oops, fuck this, time to go." The pair of them were up and running before the shot rang out. That's the thing about gunshots; they are VERY LOUD, VERY VERY LOUD. But much like a starter's pistol it just made Andy and Barbara go faster. They belted through the garden, up the side alley, across the road and didn't stop until they reached the car.

In the house Sharon was making plans.

"Car keys, now! Gwyneth, get your arse in gear."

"I'm not going anywhere."

"Fair enough."

The side of the gun hit the poor woman's temple so hard something cracked and she fell into a deep sleep. Probably troubled by dreams of Roger, however this has yet to be confirmed. The gun was pointed towards Roger once more.

"Are we ready?" Roger nodded and he was soon driving into the town centre, for some reason there were a few police cars, lights ablaze and horns on full charging up the other carriageway.

"Wonder what's going on there then?"

"No idea, Sharon; what the hell are you doing?"

"You are going to get me some money."

"Ah, well, oops, left my wallet at home."

"No you didn't I saw you put it in your pocket with the car keys."

"Worth a try."

"I will shoot you."

"I don't doubt it." Roger started to drive a little faster.

Three cars and a white van behind, Andy and Barbara were trying not to be noticed but as Roger really was starting to give the accelerator some serious welly it became obvious that they were going to lose their prey. Back at the round about, where they had first glimpsed Sharon, they saw Roger's beamer rocketing up the slip road to the bypass. There was no way she could catch up now, especially as the idiot in the white van was being such an arse. Finally past the moron and on to Roger's speedway she caught his rear end disappearing over the hill. The road wasn't too busy, rush hour had passed and the early evening traffic was flowing in precisely the manner the traffic developers had predicted, except for the mad bastard in the Beamer. Sharon wondered where it had all gone wrong. She had the gun; she should be in control. The fact that she obviously was not was pissing her off somewhat.

"Will you fucking slow down?"

"Na"

"What the hell are we doing on the bypass? I said town."

"Fuck you, what are you going to do? I've always had this theory that if some bugger pulls a gun on you, you are probably going to die. So, take said bugger with you. You shoot me now and, wee, bang smash. Both of us, well no probably you, passengers never come off that well in these situations, air bag or not. Anyway, my life as I know it is over, it's all your fault, so I may as well take it out on you, weeee." Roger gave the wheel a little wobble, as he shot by a little old lady in her little old VW.

"How's it my fault?"

"You are the one with the fucking gun you stupid cow. Oh god not the tears, the last refuge, what am I saying, the first refuge of every stupid bloody woman who wants something. Correct me if I'm wrong but; was it not you who tried to make me think I was having it away with my own daughter, was it not you who seemed to think I would be willing to cough up vast amounts of money to keep my wife in the dark?"

"You are such a shit! I can't believe I had sex with you."

"And you let me film it. Either you're a very good actress or it can't have been all that bad. Look Sharon either we are going to crash or get chased by the police, neither way looks good for you. "She made me drive like that; look she's got a gun", which incidentally looks suspiciously like a starting pistol to me. Give it up woman, for fucks sake."

Meanwhile back at the ranch, or Roger's family home, Gwyneth was awoken by the sirens and police woop woops, first came the splitting headache and then it started to come flooding back. The "Oh Shit" moment didn't really hit until she saw herself in the mirror. The "Shit, shit, shit.." moment came when the door bell rang. She cleaned up the best she could and answered the door. The two young chaps with the submachine guns looked very handsome in their uniforms. The half of her that started to flirt with them wasn't even close to being stopped by her voice of reason. She had ceased to listen to that years ago. Unfortunately she could not tell them from whence the gunshot had emanated. She was talking bollox now but at least her little voice of reason had bothered to speak up. It hadn't bothered for many years, it all seemed so pointless. Her explanation, or lack of it seemed to satisfy the two young cops and they moved their attention next door. On the other side of the road the crazy lady with all the cats was gesticulating wildly in every direction at once and shouting about how the gunshot had disturbed her furry friends. Evidently moggies emotional development suffers under the duress of gun fire. The interviewing Sergeant was just thinking about the paper work, the not inconsiderable amount of paper work, the shit loads of paper work. Gwyneth returned to the bathroom and stared at herself. The voice of reason was starting to make more sense. It was whispering in her ear about the little act of vandalism and the attempted arson, actually the actual arson and most importantly about how now would be a very good time to bugger off.

"You stupid bitch." She tried a quick smile in the mirror. It worked and she started laughing. "Time to go." Gwyneth thought about taking the fridge but it would never have fitted in her car.

 Andy and Barbara had completely lost their quarry and were about to give it all up as a bad job and go home when Roger and the weeping woman pulled up next to them at the lights. He peeped, looked across, shrugged and mouthed; " help". They followed him to the Showcase Cinema car park and pulled in next to him. Sharon was a mess of mascara and snot. The starting pistol was on the back seat.

"You should maybe hide the gun."

"It's a starting pistol."

"Had me fooled."

"Good point." Roger tucked it under the seat.

While Barbara was handing out the wet wipes and doing girl stuff with the crap kidnapper/blackmailer (but bloody good porn star) Roger was ranting on about his forthcoming speeding fines.

"Ok; I could say that there was a crazy lady in the car with a gun at my head, but then there would be loads of questions about why was there a crazy lady in the car with a gun at my head and we don't want that."

"Oh I don't know, it would be great on the news, there would be documentaries made about this. You would probably be portrayed by Trevor Eve."

Roger thought about this for a while and decided that even having the distinction of being portrayed by the great Trev was not sufficient reason to let his good name be dragged through the muck. John Nettles perhaps, but not bloody "Shoestring".

"If you have been caught on one of the many, many, many, speed cameras you flew through at several zillion miles an hour then said cameras will probably have picked up on the fact that there was a crazy lady in the car along side you with a gun at your head."

"Well she wasn't really pointing it at my head, but she did have a gun. Look this is shit; I don't want to have to explain any of this to anyone, ever! I just want it to go away. I just want you to go away." He looked back at Sharon.

"Well she did kind of blackmail you."

"And held you hostage at starting pistol point." Barbara joined in.

"I just want to go away." Sharon joined in.

"I could just call the police now and you would be taken away."

"And then you would have to explain everything to every one and you would be played by Trevor Eve in the documentary, do you really want that? Do you? I quite like Trevor Eve. I wonder who would play me?"

"But you just want to go away."

"I just want to go away."

"How fast were you going? Is there not some thing that if you go, like really fast, the camera can't catch you or something."

"Urban myth. God you would believe anything."

"Sandra Bullock."

"What."

"In the documentary, you could be Sandra Bullock."

"I'm not going to be in it, anyway she's too old for me, and she's American."

"She could have been someone he met at a conference or something, bit of international mystery, that stuff."

"Sandra Bullock is not going to be in the documentary, I'm not going to be in the documentary, there will be no documentary."

"Cheryl Cole."

"What."

"I could be Cheryl Cole."

"So I get to have it away with La Bullock and a member of Girls Aloud, sounds like fun."

"Roger, there is not going to be any bloody documentary and anyway it would be Trevor Eve not you."

"You bloody women have to spoil everything."

"What about thingy that used to play Zoe Tate in "Emmerdale", she'd be good as you."

"That's it, fuck off! There will be no documentary, coz no bugger is ever going to know, and even if there is; I shall not be in it, so sod off."

"I was thinking I could be played by David Tennant or something, that would be cool."

"You have got bugger all to do with any of this."

"What am I doing here then?"

"I don't know, wish I did. Could someone explain what this moron is doing here?"

"No money then." Sharon brought it all back home.

"Sorry, haven't got any, not that I'd give it to you anyway. Hasn't this all just got a little out of hand."

"What; you running around destroying lives, there are consequences you know, to your actions."

"Whose life? Barbara, have I ruined your life, no, didn't think so. Come off it Sharon, your life is not ruined, but we can soon change that. Of course if you would just piss off we wouldn't have to, hint, hint."

"What about Gwyneth?"

"Oh come on, she's madder than mad Missis Mad pants from mad land. Blames everyone but herself for anything untoward that happens, believes in horoscopes, all that bollox. It's hardly my fault! She's been married three times, the woman can't keep her knickers on."

"Roger, enough. Come on let's just stop this. The only person who's going to come out of this badly is you, and quite frankly that is your own bloody fault, but it will only be a speeding fine. No one needs to know about the rest of it. Good grief, if I'm the voice of reason, then things have gone a bit too far."

"Good point, well made, Andy, but; What about Gwyneth?"

"Thank you Barbara; didn't he just tell us she was Missis mad Pants."

"Ah but Chezza here twatted her with the gun, she was kind of sleepy when we left."

"Oops."

"Oops, my arse. I'm not taking the flack for that one, brain damaged and emotionally scared she may be but you may well have sent her out the other side of la la land, or killed her, whatever, and that is your problem. If I've got a choice of being dragged through the mud for being a randy old sod or going to jail for a brutal and possibly fatal assault then I'll take the "Shoestring" option. Da, na, na, na, dan, na , na, na…"

"Couldn't we just go and see if she's alright."

"Ah, the voice of reason again, what about all the police? There was a gun shot, some bugger would have heard it."

"Well I'm sorry but it is your house and you will have to go back there at some point, or do you want your wife and kids to find the rotting corpse of one of you knock offs in the front room. It's hardly an installation sculpture. You could put her in a big jar I suppose."

"Now, now kiddies: let's not fight. Chez's car is outside you house anyway, I do assume you will be wanting your car back. I'm also assuming that the back door will still be open, so, Andy you could just sneak round and have a look."

"Me being one of the two suspicious characters seen running from the scene of the crime, bugger off, you take a look. See, voice of reason, I'm getting good at this."

Roger put his phone away.

"She's not answering the phone, so she's either dead or, as Andy would say, has buggered off."

"Or is ransacking the house in a righteous fit of jealous pique…"

"Shut up Barbara."

"Piss off."

"Come on guys play nice, hey, voice of reason again, I could be a politician."

Roger made a decision, he was going back, or rather Sharon and he were going back, and if she didn't like it, tough. His explanation of her options was succinct and to the point, she came back with him voluntarily or she was going in the boot, either way until he knew what was going on with Gwyneth she was not leaving his side. Barbara and Andy decided to be brave, after all it was getting dark and perhaps no one had seen them. They would tag along behind. Sharon did find their willing-ness to go along with her being placed in the boot of Roger's car somewhat unsupportive, but as there was very little she could do at this precise moment she fell it best to just accept it. The only plan she could come up with was; RUN AWAY! But, as previously mentioned, her car was outside Roger's house of death, she could run away when they got there. The little convoy trundled at a rather less frantic speed and when they arrived there was nothing out of the ordinary to be seen what so ever. No police, no pack of reporters, no

Trevor Eve limbering up for his close ups, and certainly no Sandra Bullock, or "Sandra Fucking Bullock" as she had been referred to several times during the journey back. "Zoe Fucking Tate" also got a mention, as did Andy's rapidly diminishing chances of a shag that night. Having recently obtained his voice of reason, Andy felt it best that he should keep it safe and not waste it at this precise moment.

Anyway "Fucking Trevor Fucking Eve, are you fucking joking!" would have been a guaranteed passion killer so he kept his big fat gob shut. It had become a big fat gob fairly recently.

Roger grabbed Sharon's bag the second he pulled up, he felt sure her car keys would be in it and he didn't want her doing a runner. He was right and she didn't. The only trace of Gwyneth was a post it note on the fridge saying it was just a little too big for her car. A very happy Roger welcomed the silent twosome in and set about coffee and tea and how about a glass of wine-ing, he even found some biscuits, yum, yum. Sharon got her bag and her life back, had a cup of tea and left.

"Suppose I'll need a new cleaner then."

"Don't shag her this time."

"She could well be your daughter."

"And now that all your secret stash of home- made porn has disappeared into the either all you have to worry about is some woman you have wronged deciding to get her own back and plastering you all over the internet, with your silly little cum face,, ooh, ooh."

"Oh thanks for sharing that with me Barbara."

"Piss off."

Andy continued. "You know some buggers going to find it someday, someone will die and their kids will be looking through their stuff and there you will be, sweating and grunting and.."

"Going, ooh, ooh, ohh, with you little cum face."

"Barbara, I don't need to know about his special little cum face, really don't."

"Someone's grandchild, Mummy what's the nasty man doing to Gran?"

"And why is she wearing a school uniform?"

"Fuck off Andy, I mean do you want a lift home or not?"

"Ok, just pointing something out that I bet you never considered. "

"Fun while it lasted, oh dear, think I might take up praying."

Andy retrieved his phone and they left a somewhat relieved but also a slightly shattered Roger with his head in his hands and headed home.

"Thought you were taking me home?"

"No, we are going to mine where I am going to use you as a sex toy until I'm bored, remember. Then I'll kick you out."

"Seems fair" Andy held up his little Samsung "Want to film it? Ow! Bloody hell."

www.ingramcontent.com/pod-product-compliance
Lightning Source LLC
Chambersburg PA
CBHW031113260626
47172CB00001B/350